## "Don't start what you can't finish, honey."

He lifted his mouth from hers to mutter the warning against her lips. "If we go through with this, it's on the understanding that tomorrow no one gets to pretend it didn't happen. If you can't handle that, tell me now."

A shiver ran all the way from her heels to the top of her head, and back down again. Arching against him, Caro let her fingertips curl against the muscled wall of his chest, and pressed her nails lightly into his skin. "Don't worry about me, Gabe, worry about yourself."

She didn't know where the reckless words had come from. She knew he'd walk out of her life again. But he was never going to forget her completely. She was going to make sure of that tonight.

"Worry about myself?" There was startled humor in his eyes. "Princess, I can handle anything you dish out, and then some. I'll admit you rocked my world the last time we—"

"I didn't just rock your world, Riggs, I sent a 9.5 on the Richter scale through it," Caro retorted. "This time, I intend to bring you to your knees."

Dear Harlequin Intrigue Reader,

Those April showers go hand in hand with a welcome downpour of gripping romantic suspense in the Harlequin Intrigue line this month!

Reader-favorite Rebecca York returns to the legendary 43 LIGHT STREET with *Out of Nowhere*—an entrancing tale about a beautiful blond amnesiac who proves downright lethal to a hard-edged detective's heart. Then take a detour to New Mexico for *Shotgun Daddy* by Harper Allen—the conclusion in the MEN OF THE DOUBLE B RANCH trilogy. In this story a Navajo protector must safeguard the woman from his past who is nurturing a ticking time bomb of a secret.

The momentum keeps building as Sylvie Kurtz launches her brand-new miniseries—THE SEEKERS—about men dedicated to truth, justice…and protecting the women they love. But at what cost? Don't miss the debut book, *Heart of a Hunter*, where the search for a killer just might culminate in rekindled love. Passion and peril go hand in hand in *Agent Cowboy* by Debra Webb, when COLBY AGENCY investigator Trent Tucker races against time to crack a case of triple murder!

Rounding off a month of addictive romantic thrillers, watch for the continuation of two new thematic promotions. A handsome sheriff saves the day in *Restless Spirit* by Cassie Miles, which is part of COWBOY COPS. *Sudden Recall* by Jean Barrett is the latest in our DEAD BOLT series about silent memories that unlock simmering passions.

Enjoy all of our great offerings.

Sincerely,

Denise O'Sullivan
Senior Editor
Harlequin Intrigue

# SHOTGUN DADDY

## HARPER ALLEN

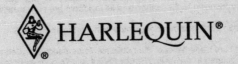

## HARLEQUIN®

TORONTO • NEW YORK • LONDON
AMSTERDAM • PARIS • SYDNEY • HAMBURG
STOCKHOLM • ATHENS • TOKYO • MILAN • MADRID
PRAGUE • WARSAW • BUDAPEST • AUCKLAND

ISBN 0-373-22766-3

SHOTGUN DADDY

Copyright © 2004 by Sandra Hill

## ABOUT THE AUTHOR

Harper Allen lives in the country in the middle of a hundred acres of maple trees with her husband, Wayne, six cats, four dogs—and a very nervous cockatiel at the bottom of the food chain. For excitement she and Wayne drive to the nearest village and buy jumbo bags of pet food. She believes in love at first sight because it happened to her.

## Books by Harper Allen

HARLEQUIN INTRIGUE
468—THE MAN THAT GOT AWAY
547—TWICE TEMPTED
599—WOMAN MOST WANTED
628—GUARDING JANE DOE*
632—SULLIVAN'S LAST STAND*
663—THE BRIDE AND THE MERCENARY*
680—THE NIGHT IN QUESTION
695—McQUEEN'S HEAT
735—COVERT COWBOY
754—LONE RIDER BODYGUARD†
760—DESPERADO LAWMAN†
766—SHOTGUN DADDY†

*The Avengers
†Men of the Double B Ranch

Don't miss any of our special offers. Write to us at the following address for information on our newest releases.

Harlequin Reader Service
U.S.: 3010 Walden Ave., P.O. Box 1325, Buffalo, NY 14269
Canadian: P.O. Box 609, Fort Erie, Ont. L2A 5X3

NEW MEXICO

Navajo
Nation

Double B
Ranch

Santa Fe

Albuquerque

Rio
Grande

Roswell

Pecos
River

N

Chihuahua
Desert

All underlined places are fictitious.

# CAST OF CHARACTERS

*Caro Moore*—She's gone from spoiled socialite to desperate single mother on the run. To save her baby from a killer, she needs the protection of the man she turned away....

*Gabe Riggs*—The Navajo hostage negotiator can't forget the one night he shared with Caro Moore. Now he's the only one who can keep her—and the baby he doesn't know is his—safe.

*Del Hawkins*—The tough ex-marine runs a boot camp ranch for bad boys—like Gabe once was. But his own past holds a dark secret that could put Gabe, Caro and their child in danger.

*Jess Crawford*—Once a Double B "bad boy," the multimillionaire has been kidnapped. Can Gabe find him before it's too late…?

*Steve Dixon*—Jess's friend and business associate. He has reasons to want Caro and her baby out of the picture for good.

*Larry Kanin*—Caro's ex-fiancé has a score to settle with Gabe. He doesn't care whom he destroys in the attempt.

*"Leo"*—The shadowy lead kidnapper has a very personal motive.

*Alice Tahe*—The Navajo matriarch knows Gabe's heritage can give him the strength to save the woman and the baby he loves. But will she convince him of that in time?

To the Simcoe Street Irregulars

# Chapter One

Gabriel Riggs got out of his rented four-wheel drive and stood beside it for a moment, going over his to-do list one final time in his mind. Fly back from Nicaragua. *Check.* Drive to Aspen. *Check.* Smash through the gate cordoning off the drive leading up the mountain to Larry Kanin's ski chalet. *Check.* There was only one item left on the list.

Find that bastard Larry and make him sorry he was ever—

"Your keys, sir? I'll park your car with the others."

Gabe frowned at the muscular young man confronting him. In the light from the Olympic-style torches lining the drive, the security guard's fresh face contrasted with the commando-like gear he was wearing. The guard's eyes narrowed.

"Wait a minute. Are you on the guest list?"

"No."

Gabe headed past him toward the redwood steps ascending to the veranda. Kanin's man grabbed his arm. "If you're not on the list, you're going to have to be escorted off the—"

Get past Security. *Check.*

Gabe crossed the veranda, not bothering to look back at the sprawled figure in the snow behind him. That was Larry all over, he thought savagely. All style and no substance, even down to the beefcake he had guarding his own property. But hell, when all someone cared about was the bottom line, maybe style was all it took. Recoveries International's corporate clientele roster grew every time Kanin attended a function flanked by his six-and-a-half-foot blond robots.

Probably even Tech-Oil Consolidated would stay with the firm. After all, the death of one of their employees at the hands of kidnappers had saved them a bundle.

The noise hit him as he entered the chalet—a raucous mix of laughter, too-loud music and brittle voices. He'd heard about the beautiful people, Gabe thought, scanning the room and taking in the cluster of après-skiers by the fireplace, the group near a buffet table. He guessed that was who these people were, but Kanin wasn't among them. He switched his attention to a redhead who was favoring him with an appraising glance.

"Where's Larry?"

"Who cares?" Her hair looked as if she'd just gotten out of bed, but maybe it was supposed to look that way. "I love the silver cuff you're wearing, handsome. It's Apache, isn't it?"

At the far side of the room an open set of polished wood stairs swept in a large curve to a second floor. Kanin had to be upstairs.

Gabe shook his head. "Navajo."

It was an effort to make even that much conversation. He tried to tell himself that what he was feeling was jet lag, or exhaustion from going the past three days without sleep, but he knew it wasn't either of those. These people and their world meant nothing to him. He was here only to settle an account.

He put his foot on the bottommost stair. He looked up and saw the woman, and for half a heartbeat all else fell away.

She was like ice and snow and crystals, he thought, his chest feeling suddenly too tight. Her eyes were the color of an alpine lake, her hair a silvery blond pulled back from the creamy oval of her face and coiled at the nape of her neck. She was wearing a white sweater, white slim-fitting ski pants, small white boots with heels. A full-length coat of some kind of white fur hung from her shoulders.

Even as she swept down the staircase toward him, Larry Kanin appeared at the top of the stairs behind her.

Oxygen slammed back into Gabe's lungs.

"For God's sake, Caro, you're overreacting." Kanin's well-cut lips tightened. "So Jinx and I were having a little fun. It didn't mean anything."

The woman stopped halfway down the stairs. "This is what doesn't mean anything anymore, Larry."

Swiftly she removed a blazing diamond from one finger and flung it over the heads of the guests below. The ring sparkled over the buffet table and landed in a bowl of salmon mousse.

But the woman Kanin had called Caro didn't wait

to see it fall. Gabe just had time to step aside before she moved by him, her head held high and those starry eyes not registering his existence. The fur of her coat brushed coldly against his arm, the faint scent that enveloped her—it smelled like small white flowers, he thought disjointedly—touched him briefly, and then she was past. He heard the front door open and close.

Kanin had followed Caro part of the way down the stairs, and for a moment Gabe thought he meant to go after her. Then Larry shrugged, the anger in his eyes quickly concealed.

"I promised entertainment, didn't I?" he drawled to his assembled guests. "Whichever one of you ladies finds that ring first gets to keep it."

There was a chorus of surprised laughter from the females in his party and a general rumble of amusement from the men. The buffet table was instantly surrounded.

"Hi, Larry."

Kanin had been watching the stampede that his announcement had started. At Gabe's greeting, his gaze swung away from his guests.

"God—Riggs! What the hell are you doing here?"

"The same thing your woman just did." Gabe mounted the steps that divided them. "I'm breaking up with you, Larry."

Kanin frowned. "This isn't the time or the place, Riggs. We'll talk at the office on—"

"They weren't asking much in the first place. When I reported in by phone I told you I was pretty sure we'd be able to get it down to a quarter-mill, tops.'' Gabe looked over at the buffet table. ''I don't get it. You just turned close to that amount into a party favor.''

''For Christ—'' Kanin's jaw tightened. ''I recommended Tech-Oil draw a line in the sand, all right? They do a lot of business in volatile regions, and if they got the reputation of being patsies for every guerrilla leader looking to fund his war chest, they'd be out of business in a month.''

''So instead of advising Tech-Oil to increase security for its people, you told them to stall on delivering the good-faith payment to the kidnappers.'' Gabe nodded. ''I just needed to hear you confirm it. Like I said, we're through. And since I don't have a diamond to throw over this banister—''

The buffet table broke Kanin's fall before tipping completely over, and the last sight Gabe had of him was of a chafing dish of tiny meatballs upending itself over Kanin as he lay among the debris.

Outside, the baby Nazi he'd decked was nowhere to be seen. He opened the door of his rental vehicle and smelled small white flowers.

''I need a ride into Aspen.'' She was sitting in the passenger seat, her hands clasped tightly in her lap and her gaze fixed straight ahead. ''I want to leave now.''

The baby Nazi might be out of the picture, Gabe thought, but any minute now, reinforcements would arrive. He didn't have time to argue with her. He slid into the driver's seat.

''No problem, lady,'' he said tersely. ''I don't want to hang around here any longer, either.''

The spell he'd fallen under when he'd first laid eyes on her had been broken, he noted in relief. She was still beautiful, still a snow princess, and he didn't mind helping her out by giving her a ride. But breaking off her engagement to Larry couldn't change the fact that she belonged in his world of wealth and arrogance. The coolness behind her demand just now was proof of that.

Being able to breathe around her made things easier, he told himself as he negotiated the litter of broken wood that had once been the gate at the bottom of the slope. He turned to her when he was safely past it.

"I've got to turn on the heat. You might want to take off that fur."

All he could see of her was the back of her head as she stared out of the side window at the gathering darkness. "I'm not cold."

"I am." He reached forward and switched on the heater, jacking the fan to full speed. "I haven't acclimatized yet."

She turned to frown at him before opening the coat and slipping her arms from its sleeves. "When I saw your vehicle parked and running in the drive, I assumed one of Larry's guests was leaving early—but you weren't at the party, were you."

Her question sounded faintly accusatory. He kept his face expressionless.

"The name's Gabriel Riggs. You're right, I wasn't invited, but I showed up anyway. You walked past me after you tossed your engagement ring into the salmon mousse. Larry landed in the same general vicinity a couple of minutes later.''

The four-wheel drive corrected itself on a curve. Gabe exchanged the high-beams for the regular headlights to cut down on the hypnotizing dazzle of the now-swirling snow.

''You threw him off the stairs? Why?''

''Because of a man named Leo Roswell. Your ex-lover let him get his throat cut, honey.'' He glanced at her. ''It was a Recoveries International situation that went real bad, real fast, but I was the negotiator on the spot. I should have guessed Larry might think it was a good idea to pull the plug.''

''A man got his throat—'' She didn't finish the sentence. He heard her indrawn breath. ''That's horrible.''

Gabe didn't know why he'd put it so bluntly. He didn't even know why he was talking to her about it. ''Yeah, it was horrible. So did you walk in on Larry with Jink, or whatever her name was?''

''Jinx. I don't want to discuss it.'' The frosty tone was back in full force. Gabe took the hint, and for the better part of the next hour there was nothing but silence between them—a silence that was finally broken by Caro herself when his arm accidentally brushed against hers as he reached for the stick shift. She stiffened. ''How long before we get to Aspen?''

The lady might as well have posted No Trespassing signs, Gabe thought. It was obvious not only that she wasn't interested in having a conversation, but that she was having second thoughts about being in his company at all. To be fair, he couldn't really blame her for her show of nerves just now. He had a pretty good idea of what she saw when she looked at him— a big man with straight black hair that should have been cut two weeks ago and an outdoor-worker's tan deepening his natural copper, wearing faded jeans and a thin cotton shirt. Not at all what she'd been expecting when she'd made the snap decision to hop into his waiting vehicle outside the chalet.

And if she wasn't enthralled with having him as a travelling companion, he thought wryly, she was going to be real thrilled about bunking in with him tonight.

"Change of plans," he said, narrowing his gaze against the heavy snow and wondering if he'd already passed the place he was looking for. "We're not making Aspen—not till morning, at least. This blizzard's getting worse. We're going to have to find somewhere to hole up for the night."

Her gaze was arctic. "Stay the night with a man I met an hour ago? If that's supposed to be a joke, I don't see the humor—and if it isn't, you've made a big mistake, Mr. Riggs. The driving can't be that bad. We'll keep going."

Ignoring her peremptory order, Gabe saw the laneway he'd noticed earlier in the day when he'd been heading the other way. He eased his foot onto the brake, thought for a tense moment that the vehicle was going to lose it on the patch of glare ice that appeared suddenly in his headlights, and then made the turn. Gravel crunched under the tires as they took a slight incline to the darkened building ahead.

"A weekend lodge like this, they've probably got

an alarm system.'' He brought the four-wheel drive to a stop, looked at her stiff figure and took the keys from the ignition. ''Trust me, we wouldn't have made it, and if it's your reputation you're worrying about, don't. I'm going to disable the security, so even if the cops could get here in these conditions, they won't have a need to.''

Her eyes lasered through him. ''I don't want to be here. I don't want to spend the night with you. My father's William Moore, and if that name doesn't mean anything to you, it should. Turn this car around right now.''

It had been a long day—hell, a long week, Gabe reflected tightly. Even when he'd been busy throwing Larry over the banister he hadn't allowed himself to lose the numbness that had surrounded him since he'd seen Leo Roswell's dead body. He'd known that a single spark of emotion would be enough to blaze down the flimsy barriers holding back his emotions.

Caro Moore had just lit that spark. He tried to count to ten, gave up at seven, and got out of the car. He went around to her door and opened it.

''Drop the lady-of-the-manor act, honey, and pronto. I'm not your chauffeur. I'm getting real tired of you treating me like one. Get out of the car.''

''Didn't you hear what I just—''

The rest of her sentence was lost in a gasp as he lifted her from the car seat and deposited her unceremoniously into one of the snowdrifts beside the vehicle. He looked down at her.

''Let's get things straight, princess. You're a rich bitch. I'm some version of hired muscle. You obviously think that means I can't wait to have my crude way with you, but at the risk of shattering your illusions, I'm not interested.'' He forced an evenness into his tone. ''I'll help you up.''

''I don't need your help,'' she retorted, her heeled boots choosing that moment to slip on a patch of ice.

He reached down and hauled her to her feet—too roughly, he realized as he became momentarily unbalanced.

Only the fact that his vehicle was behind him saved them both from losing their footing. Furious blue eyes met his from a distance of only a few inches as Caro slammed against him.

''You're the one with the illusions, Mr. Riggs—'' Her lips, pale pink and way too close, bit off the words. ''Am I supposed to believe this wasn't planned, either? Let go of me.''

''My pleasure.'' He released his grip on her, hoping that nothing of what was going through his mind showed in his face.

The breathlessness he'd felt when he'd first seen her was back worse than ever, he thought hollowly, and it didn't matter that she was too rich, too arrogant and too damn spoiled. Just for an instant he imagined how she'd look beneath him, that pale hair spread out on the snow, those pale lips parted—

He turned away quickly, his fists clenched at his sides. ''Wait here. This shouldn't take long.''

Whoever the lodge's owners were, they were like Kanin; their security system had all the bells and whistles. But one snip through a wire made it useless. It was the same with the dead bolt on their front door.

Gabe jimmied it open and walked back to the car, but by the time he'd locked the vehicle, he saw her slim figure, her back ramrod straight under the fur coat she'd slipped into again, entering the house.

He leaned against the four-by-four and dragged his hand across his mouth.

What the hell was the matter with him? Caro Moore was no different from any of the wealthy socialites with whom he'd come into contact in his job. She expected to snap her fingers and have someone jump. She'd never worked for a living, had never had to worry about the rent, had never ventured out of her shallow little circle of similarly wealthy friends and acquaintances.

She didn't live in his world. He had no desire to live in hers. How hard could it be not to let the woman get to him?

Hard enough, he admitted grimly as he entered the house and saw her standing in front of an empty fireplace. She gave no indication that she was aware of his presence, and he squelched the flicker of irritation that rose in him.

"There's a woodpile at the side of the house," he said in as neutral a tone as he could muster. "I'd better bring some in to keep us going if we lose the electricity."

She didn't turn around. "The phone doesn't work. You did something to it when you sabotaged the security, didn't you."

He'd tried, dammit, Gabe thought, not even bothering to count to ten this time. He'd cut her all the

slack he had available, but now he'd come to the end
of the line.

With two strides he closed the space between them.
He spun her around to face him, and saw surprise
replace some of the icy hauteur in her gaze.

"How'd you guess, honey?" he said through
clenched teeth. "Yeah, it's all part of my big bad
plan—the weather, the phones, finding this place and
breaking in. So how about it? You and me, the snow
princess and the hired hand—wanna get it on? Hey,
I'm not your fiancé, but that's probably a plus right
now, as far as you're concerned."

He saw a small white-gloved hand blurring toward
his face. He caught her wrist just as her palm kissed
his cheek.

"No, sweetheart," he said, his smile crooked. "I
don't play rough with women, and I don't let them
play rough with me. Let's both stop with the games,
okay?"

He lowered her hand without releasing her wrist,
regret already setting in. "I shouldn't have yanked
your chain like I did just now. We're stuck with each
other for the night, so why don't we call a truce? I'm
willing if you are."

Her gaze locked on his, as if she were determining
whether she could trust him. Those silky dark lashes
didn't have mascara on them, he noted. In fact, she
wasn't wearing any kind of makeup that he could see.
Her skin was naturally creamy. Her lips were naturally a pale pink shade. Her eyes were naturally a
deep, heartbreaking blue that could make a man's
mouth go dry and his knees buckle beneath—

"You really stopped because the road was getting too dangerous?" Her uncertain question broke through his musings.

"Yeah, princess, I did. On a job a few years ago I was forced to ride shotgun on a Jeep carrying a load of dynamite through the jungle, and believe me, I felt safer then than I did tonight trying to avoid those patches of black ice." He felt tension seep out of her. "So are we good here?"

Her eyes still on his, she gave the tiniest of nods. He relaxed his hold on her wrist.

The next moment he rocked back on his heels as her palm connected solidly with his cheek.

"Are we *good* here? After you made that crack about how I must feel toward the man I was going to marry?" Her glare was blue fire. "This evening I walked in on Larry while he and another woman were indulging in a variation of 'getting it on,' as you'd probably put it. When he realized he'd been caught, he told me that if I'd ever shown any interest in performing that particular act on him, he wouldn't have *had* to cheat on me. Do you have any idea how humiliating tonight was for me? Do you think I like knowing that when I get back to Albuquerque, everyone's going to be whispering about what Larry's prude of a fiancée does and doesn't do in the bedroom?"

Pain flashed behind her eyes. She blinked it away. "So, no, we're *not* good here. I'd sooner spend the night in the car than another minute with you."

She began to push past him. Instinctively Gabe put out a hand to stop her, nudging the fur coat from her shoulders as he did. He grasped her lightly, his fingers spread wide on the soft whiteness of her sweater.

"You're right, I was way out of line." Her lips tightened at his words, but he saw past the dismissive gesture to the tightly wound tension she'd hidden so well.

Or perhaps Caro Moore hadn't had to hide it that well, he told himself slowly. Maybe he'd been so preoccupied with his failure to save a hostage that he hadn't wanted to notice the woman behind the icy facade.

Sure, she had attitude. She had it in spades. But pampered princess or not, she hadn't deserved to learn the way she had what a jerk Kanin was.

"If anyone's bunking in the car tonight, I am," he said. "I owe you that, at least, and I'm used to sleeping rough."

He let his hands slide from her shoulders. Even as he did he saw the twin smears of black grease they left against the pristine white of her cashmere sweater. Caro's eyes widened in appalled disbelief as she saw them, too.

*Sweet move, Riggs,* Gabe thought, his heart sinking. Suddenly he felt he was everything she believed him to be—coarse, crude, and better suited to being in a mechanic's bay working on her car than standing here trying to talk to her—or hell, touch her. He began to apologize, knew there was nothing she wanted to hear from him, and shrugged in defeat.

"You realize that won't come out," she said in a tight voice. She didn't take her gaze off the finger-prints running from her shoulders to just above the curve of her breasts. "You realize that's probably gone right through the fabric."

"The alarm box was humidity-proofed with packing grease." Without meaning to, he followed her gaze. "I must have gotten it on my hands when I was disconnecting the wires."

He stepped away from her rigid figure, wondering if it was his imagination or if he'd suddenly become bigger, bulkier, more awkward. He still couldn't seem to avert his eyes from the agitated rise and fall of her breasts.

"I'd better get the hell out of here before I completely mess you up," he muttered, taking another slow step away.

With an effort he began to drag his gaze from her. Caro slipped a gloved finger under the neckline of the sweater and pulled it slightly away from her body. She let the soft wool fall back into place and looked up at him.

"I'll probably need some kind of abrasive soap to clean it off my skin."

Her voice was still tight, but now there seemed to be a breathiness to it, he thought in confusion. Or maybe he was projecting, he told himself. Yeah. That had to be it.

"Pumice," he said thickly. "When I've been working on an engine I have to scrub my nails with pumice. But that's probably too rough."

"If rough works, I'll try it." He hadn't imagined the breathiness. Her eyes were wide and locked on his. "I can't go around like this, can I? I have to scrub it away somehow."

She wasn't talking about cleaning abrasives any-more, he realized with sudden certainty. He shook his head and tried to take another step backward. The small heels of her boots clicked against the floor as she took three steps forward and stopped in front of him.

"After tomorrow I don't imagine I'll ever see you again." Her lips barely moved as she spoke. Slowly she brought a fingertip to his chest and traced the rim of one of his shirt buttons, her attention seemingly focused on the small action. "You'll drop me off in Aspen in the morning and it'll be like tonight never happened."

Gabe swallowed. "That's not how it would be, princess," he said, too hoarsely. "I don't think you're the type that can tell herself it didn't happen. I think you'd remember everything, whether you wanted to or not."

He turned away. "You'd better get some sleep. I'll see you in the morning."

He'd never known his father, but he knew his mother had been Navajo. *Stoicism. Big Dineh quality,* he told himself, mentally using the Navajo term rather than the Anglo one. *Hell, maybe I'll be thankful later, but right now I can't believe I'm walking away from her.*

But he didn't have a choice—not if he wanted to be able to look himself in the mirror tomorrow.

She wanted to prove something to herself, though she didn't have to. Kanin had seen a vulnerability beneath that cool exterior and had aimed his jab right at the place where it would hurt the most. The bastard had made her feel it was her fault he'd gone to another woman for the sexual favor he'd wanted performed on him. Tomorrow Caro Moore would be able to see her ex-fiancé's accusation for what it was—a cheap shot from a man who didn't deserve her. But tonight, she was in pain and she wanted to scrub away the humiliation as harshly as possible.

*And she was going to use you to do it, buddy,* the small voice in Gabe's head said firmly. *You don't wanna play stud for a spoiled little socialite, right?*

The hell he didn't. But he wasn't going to. And that was final.

He'd almost made it to the door when her voice stopped him.

"I don't look like I'm all ice, but I must be. That has to be why you're turning me down—because you can tell just by looking at me that it wouldn't be any good for you. Is that what you see, Gabe? Am I so obviously frozen?"

He turned around, and knew as soon as he had that he'd made a mistake. She'd pulled off the white sweater. Under it she was wearing a lacy white bra—*of course,* Gabe thought dizzily—and she'd been right, some of the lace was smudged. More dark prints stood out against the creamy swell of her breasts.

He wasn't aware that he'd moved, but somehow he was right in front of her. "Maybe a little frozen," he rasped. "I kind of like that, though."

"Then, how can you walk away?" The pain in her voice was almost his undoing. "It must be me. Larry was right."

"He was wrong." He forced himself to keep his

hands at his sides. "If you really want to know what I see when I look at you, I'll tell you. I see that lush mouth and I wonder what it would be like to have it on me; I see that pale hair and think of it falling across your face while you call out my name. I see heat that could sear a brand onto a man. But I won't take advantage of how you feel tonight, Caro. I don't think I could live with myself if I did."

"And I don't think I'll be able to stand it if you don't," she whispered.

His hands were shaking, dammit. He raised his left one from his side, the heavy silver and turquoise cuff glinting coldly against the tan of his arm. He brought his palm to within a hairbreadth of that pale, smudged skin—and stopped.

Her teeth sunk into her bottom lip. Her mouth bloomed dark pink. It looked like a single rose petal floating on cream.

"I don't care," she said with low fierceness. "Don't you understand? I *want* to see where you've been on me."

Heat slammed through Gabe. He pressed his outspread hand over her breast, let his thumb slip under the chaste lace of her no-longer white bra, dragged the flimsy fabric downward.

"I shouldn't be doing this, princess," he said unsteadily.

As if of its own volition, his right hand slid past her hips to cup the curves of that tight, white-clad rump. He lifted her to him, one-handedly held her against him, felt the shock that ran through her as she was forced to wrap her legs around his waist to steady herself. With his other hand he pulled a clip from the coil at the nape of her neck, and as her hair fell free he spread his fingers against the back of her head. He kept them there and kissed her.

It was like falling into a world of snow, like being buried in snow, like *burning* in snow. The smell of white and the taste of white—white flowers and white heat—flamed across his soul.

She'd wanted his mark on her. He wanted hers on him, he thought, raw desire spilling through him.

And a few minutes later as he sank to his knees on the snowy fur, Caro Moore's arms and legs entwined around him and her mouth under his, Gabriel Riggs surrendered himself to the cold flames and the burning ice and the woman who needed him for only one night....

# Chapter Two

Even with the SUV's air-conditioning as high as it could go and the sleeveless dress she was wearing no more than a breath of silk against her skin, Caro felt as if she was burning up. If what Jess Crawford had told her before he'd left for Mexico a few days ago was right and he'd finally run his old friend to earth here in an isolated corner of New Mexico's Chihuahua Desert, in a short while she'd be seeing Gabriel Riggs again.

It had been eighteen months since the night she'd spent with him. She was almost certain he would take one look at her and tell her to go to hell.

*He'd be well within his rights if he did,* she told herself. *Even if you can't remember the exact words you threw at him when you and he parted ways in Aspen the next morning, you know they were—*

Abruptly she cut off the comforting lie before she could take it further. The truth was, she remembered everything—the words, the cutting tone in which she'd delivered them, and the desperate pride that had prompted her unforgivable outburst.

She'd awoken in his arms that morning a year and

a half ago, unable at first to identify the unfamiliar emotion filling her. Only after she'd looked at a still-sleeping Gabe beside her had she been able to put a name to what she was feeling.

Total contentment. Total happiness. And the ridiculous but undeniable conviction that no matter how it had come about, she'd somehow found the one man in the world she would ever want.

She didn't know how long she lay there watching him sleep. She only knew that as she did she found herself wanting to slide her fingers through the tangle of blue-black hair obscuring his closed eyes, wanting to trace the assorted scars on his tough hide and ask him how he'd gotten each one. When she realized what she was thinking, doubt flickered skittishly through her. She tried to tell herself that her world and his were too different, that he was nothing more than hired muscle, that what had passed between them had been merely physical—a rash one-night fling she already regretted.

It didn't work. And with a flash of devastating self-knowledge she understood that the woman she'd been twenty-four hours ago—a woman to whom shallow reasons like those would have mattered—was gone for good.

"You look appalled, princess."

Still trying to assimilate the shattering revelation she'd had, she didn't realize he'd opened his eyes and was looking at her until he spoke. Before she could reply, he slid his arm out from under her and got to his feet.

"Don't be. This never happened, remember?"

Raking his hair back, he gave her a tight smile. "This never happened, I won't call you, and you don't have to worry about running into me again. That's the upside of sleeping with a loner, honey. Men like me don't stick around long enough to become a problem."

For a moment she refused to believe that the words were coming from the same man who'd whispered her name all night, who'd held her gaze with his as the two of them had urged each other to ecstasy only hours earlier. He shrugged, and the gesture pierced Caro more than his comments had.

"Men like you?" Her voice came out in a croak, but he didn't seem to notice.

"Yeah, princess, men like me. You know—rough-and-ready types who don't know what fork to use at those white-tie dinners you have, who would be told to use the back entrance if they showed up at your rich daddy's Albuquerque mansion, who take on the dirty jobs your social circle doesn't want to admit exist...like dealing with kidnappers. You had me pegged from the minute I told you we were going to spend the night here together, and that look I saw in your eyes a few minutes ago made it pretty obvious you woke up with second thoughts about what we did last night." His tone took on an edge. "You *were* having second thoughts, am I right?"

"Second thoughts? Heavens, no."

She was amazed to hear the amused astonishment in her tone—amazed and grateful. Because everything depended on pulling off the act she wanted him to buy, Caro told herself—her self-esteem, her ability to get past this moment without falling apart, her pride.

"Last night satisfied my curiosity, Gabe. You said it yourself—I see men like you doing work around my father's estate, or as hired security at a function. My girlfriends and I've always thought it might be thrilling in a naughty way to spend a night with that type of man." She forced a laugh. "You were a fantasy come true, and it was even kind of fun having to persuade you, but you're right—the ground rules still stand. It would be embarrassing for both of us if you showed up on my doorstep in the mistaken belief that this had been anything more than it was."

She tipped her head to one side. "This never happened, you won't call me, and I don't have to worry about running into you again. Promise?"

"Sure," he said tonelessly. "But the next time you get curious, honey, consider calling an agency who sends the kind of man you're looking for out on house calls. That way you won't have to worry about any misunderstandings at all."

The drive to Aspen had been conducted in near-total silence, Caro remembered now. Gabe had dropped her off in front of a five-star hotel, she'd checked into a suite, and after drawing herself a bath so hot that billows of perfumed steam rose from the tub, she'd immersed herself in a vain attempt to melt the core of ice that seemed to have formed inside her.

The ice hadn't melted—not then, and not upon her return to Albuquerque, where she'd informed her father that she'd broken off her engagement to a man he'd seen as an eminently suitable prospective husband for her. It hadn't melted over the following weeks during the rounds of parties she'd forced herself to attend. And then one day she'd frowned at the calendar, made a quick calculation, and had felt the first hairline fissure appear in the numbness she'd begun to think had become a permanent part of her.

A few days later she'd shakily dialed the number she'd obtained for Gabe. He was going to be a father. She was carrying his child. Surely opening the conversation with a bombshell like that would catch him off guard enough that he would listen to the rest of what she had to tell him—that he'd misinterpreted the dismay he'd seen on her face when he'd awoken that morning, that a lifetime of being Caroline Moore, daughter of a man who'd taught her from childhood that emotions were to be concealed, had caused her to clutch at her pride instead of revealing her true feelings.

"I would have poured it all out to him if he'd still been there to answer that phone call," Caro said out loud, her hands gripping the SUV's wheel and her gaze fixed on the empty desert landscape rushing by. But he hadn't been. It had all been true on his part— Gabe Riggs was a loner who didn't stick around long enough to have relationships. She was glad she had found out before the baby was born. No child needed a father who'd rather be somewhere else, instead of tied down to a woman he had no fond memories of and a baby he hadn't planned on.

Which made her current quest all the more ironic, she thought tensely. Because right now the only man who could help her was the one man she'd assumed she would never see—

She hit the SUV's brakes to avoid whizzing past the gas station she'd been told to watch for. It was no wonder she'd nearly missed the building, she thought as she maneuvered around a truck that had been abandoned beside what remained of a pair of gasoline pumps. The structure was close to being a ruin. No one had lived here for decades.

Jess's information had to be wrong.

Caro brought the sports utility to a stop, tears of disappointment and fear pricking at the back of her eyes. Even as her vision blurred she blinked the tears back.

At one end of the ramshackle building a rusty nail protruded from a broken board. Slung from the nail was what she'd first taken as a rag but on second glance proved to be a shirt. It wasn't faded enough to have been hanging there for years.

She opened the door, stepped out of the vehicle and walked to the side of the building.

He was standing beneath an oil drum that had obviously been rigged up as a primitive shower. Water was sprinkling down through holes punched into the bottom of the drum. He was lean muscle and whipcord sinews and bronzed hide. He was completely naked.

Caro's breath caught in her throat. She put her hand on the side of the building to steady herself.

Gabe looked over his shoulder and his gaze met hers. ''Don't come another step closer,'' he said flatly.

She'd expected hostility from him, she acknowledged numbly. She hadn't expected the piercing pain that demolished her already-shaky defences at this curt evidence that whatever Gabe Riggs might once have felt for her was dead and gone.

He reached up to the side of the oil drum and, before she understood what he was doing, he brought down a sawed-off shotgun, braced it one-handedly against his body and pulled the trigger. Out of the corner of her eye she saw splinters fly explosively from the side of the building as the heavy body of a greenish-colored snake gave one last, headless spasm a few feet away from where she stood frozen in her tracks. It was a moment before she could trust herself to speak.

''I—I think you just saved my life.'' Her voice wasn't entirely steady, but she hoped he would put the quaver in her tone down to what had just happened.

''Since that was a Mojave rattler, I think I did, too.''

As Gabe replaced the shotgun in a sling at the side of the oil drum, she saw a gleam of silver on his left wrist and recognized the bracelet he'd worn the night they'd met. With no self-consciousness at all, he ducked his head under the final trickle of water before stepping away from the patch of already-drying earth under his makeshift shower and picking up a pair of patched khakis. He put them on, raked wet hair out of his eyes and retrieved the shotgun, then walked past her.

"How did you find me?" As he spoke he kept walking, while shrugging his shoulders into his shirt.

"Through an old friend of yours, Jess Crawford. I met him once or twice at parties when I was dating Larry. I work for him now, as his social secretary." She resisted the impulse to look away. "My situation's changed since we last met, Gabe, but that's not relevant. Jess needs your help. From what I gather, he and you go back a long way."

"Fifteen years." Gabe's jaw tightened. "Did ol' Jess feed you a line about the crazy times we had together with Tyler Adams and Virge Connor at the Double B Ranch, when we were sent there as juvenile delinquents to turn our lives around? Did he credit the fact that he's now a software billionaire and a solid citizen to Del Hawkins, the ex-marine who runs the ranch and whipped us into shape?"

She stared at him, disconcerted. "Not in so many words, but yes. He told me that being sent to the Double B was the best thing that ever happened to him. He said all four of you felt that way."

"Jess is a nice guy. His problem's always been in believing that wanting something bad enough makes it come true." Gabe shrugged. "If it's a Double B band-of-brothers reunion Jess wants me to attend, tell him thanks but no thanks. And tell him to come himself the next time he needs a favor."

He opened the SUV's door. "Expensive vehicle, expensive-looking dress, and those strappy little sandals you're wearing probably cost more than I used to make in a week before I quit Recoveries International. It doesn't look to me as if your situation's changed that much, even if you are filling in time by playing secretary for Jess. You're still a snow princess. Better be on your way before that creamy skin starts to burn.''

She couldn't afford to take offence at his tone, but a spark of desperate anger flared in her nonetheless.

''Maybe the changes in my life just don't seem so significant in comparison to your situation.'' She gazed steadily at him. ''Why did you disappear, Gabe? Was it because you blamed yourself for Leo Roswell's death?''

''Leo's death was why I stopped being a hostage negotiator. I knew that if I hadn't seen what Kanin was planning, the instincts I'd always relied on were gone.'' His smile was brief. ''As for why I dropped off the face of the earth, I don't see how that's any of your damn business, sweetheart.''

''Then I'd better stick to what *is* my business. I'm here because Jess once told me that if he was ever kidnapped, the only man he'd trust to negotiate his release would be you.''

The sunlight was so strong that Gabe's eyes seemed a translucent amber, but just for a moment they deepened to black. She saw his jaw tighten as he took in what she hadn't said.

''When and where?''

For the first time since she'd found him here in this nowhere spot Caro allowed her emotions to show. ''Two days ago, just across the border in Mexico. His abductors snatched him while he was down there supervising construction of a new Crawford Solutions plant he's having built.'' She shook her head. ''Oh,

Gabe—Jess's business partner Steve Dixon called in Kanin's firm to handle negotiations for his release. I'm afraid something's going to go wrong.''

''If Recoveries International's been hired, even if I wanted to I wouldn't be able to involve myself.'' His tone was flat. ''I wouldn't have the authority to replace—''

''But that's just it—I do,'' she interrupted. ''I told you I was Jess's social secretary. That's true, as far as it goes, but our relationship's grown over the year and a half I've been working for him. A few weeks ago he asked me to marry him.''

He looked away. ''Congratulations, but I don't—''

''I said I needed time to think it over, but he still insisted on signing some document that gave me power of attorney over his affairs, which is why my choice of hostage negotiator will take precedence over Steve Dixon's. I won't lie to you, Gabe—I've decided I'm going to tell him I accept his proposal. But first I need your help to bring him home.''

His expression closed. ''Jess deserves a negotiator who'll give him a fighting chance to come out of this alive, not a burned-out case who could get him killed.''

''He deserves the man he asked for when he first suspected this day might come—'' she retorted, ''the man he has faith in. You're that man, Gabe, whether you like it or not. Maybe you've been able to walk away from the rest of the world, but you can't walk away from one of your oldest friends.''

''No?'' His smile was humorless. ''Just watch me, princess.''

She'd gambled and lost, Caro thought dully. But what had she expected? Gabriel Riggs had once called her a rich bitch, and the morning after they'd slept together she'd done everything she could to convince him that his assessment of her had been correct. She'd been insane to think that a plea for help from her would mean anything to him.

"You said Jess suspected this day might come." About to turn away, he paused. "What made him think he was in danger of being kidnapped?"

"Nothing specific," she said tonelessly. "Just the feeling once or twice that he was being followed. But when I suggested he hire a bodyguard, he told me he'd never wanted his wealth to curtail his life and he wasn't going to start now. I guess that attitude made it easy for his kidnappers. The one who phoned to tell us they had Jess certainly seemed to think so."

"You're leaving something out." His gaze sharpened. "What aren't you telling me?"

He wanted the truth from her—the whole truth, Caro thought. He wanted more than she was prepared to give.

"The kidnapper who called said we'd better make sure nothing went wrong," she said unevenly. "He said that not only was Jess's life at stake, but that if they had to kill him they'd come after me and my baby daughter, Emily."

She saw his eyes darken in shock and answered his question before he could ask it, knowing that her child's whole world depended on convincing him.

"Emily is Larry's baby, Gabe," she lied, her gaze clear and unwavering on his. "I was already pregnant with her when I met you eighteen months ago, but before you try to tell me that as her father he'll want to take sole responsibility for her safety, you should know that I've never told him what his relationship is to her—and I don't intend to.''

She shook her head. ''I told you my circumstances had changed. I've changed, too. I'll do whatever I have to, to give my daughter a happy and secure life. Larry wasn't fiancé material, and he's not father material, either. Even if Jess hadn't offered me a job and a place to live after my father disowned me, I still wouldn't have approached Kanin for any kind of support in return for letting him play a part in Emmie's life.''

''Your father disowned you?'' He frowned. ''Because you were pregnant, for God's sake?''

''Because I was pregnant and I wouldn't say who the father was. All I told him was that it wasn't Larry. Father had been upset enough over the breakup of my engagement. If he'd known it was Larry's child I was carrying, he would have bulldozed a marriage through, no matter what.''

She tried to smile. ''William Moore always gets what he wants. As soon as he realized that this time he wasn't going to, he told me he no longer considered me his daughter. When I ran into Jess a few weeks later, I'd just been fired from my third job in a row and I was at my wit's end as to how I was going to survive. I'm not a princess anymore, Gabe, I'm a working single mom.''

''With a marriage proposal from a software billionaire.'' There was nothing in Gabe's voice but detachment. ''When's the handover scheduled for?''

''Sometime tonight. The Crawford Solutions jet will get us to Jess's Mexican villa in under an hour, and we're to be contacted there with the exact time and place. Steve Dixon's flying down with me, although Larry and a contingent of his men are already at the villa.''

''Larry took a contingent of his men? How many is a contingent, exactly?''

Caro blinked. ''I don't know, ten or twelve. Why?''

''Because you don't need an army to hand over a ransom, for God's sake,'' Gabe replied tersely. ''You only need an army if you intend to stage a battle. Kanin's going to pull some kind of cowboy stunt, dammit.''

''But—'' She felt the blood drain from her face. ''But that could get Jess killed,'' she whispered, appalled. ''And then his kidnappers will come after Emily, just as they threatened to.''

The desert heat and the blazing sun seemed suddenly replaced by a bone-numbing cold and a darkness so total it might have been deadest night. She couldn't let anything happen to her daughter, Caro told herself in desperation—she *wouldn't* let anything happen.

No matter what she had to offer him, she needed to convince Gabe to take control of the hostage negotiation. But what could she offer a man who'd turned his back on everything?

The same thing she'd offered Gabriel Riggs once before to persuade him to go against his better judgment, she thought shakily. Herself. Because even if he didn't like her, even if his opinion of her character was that she was still a shallow, spoiled princess, he'd once wanted her so badly that for one night he hadn't been able to get enough of her, just as she hadn't been able to get enough of him.

For a moment she almost lost her nerve. Only the thought of what was at stake gave her the courage to go on.

"You once told me that when you looked at my mouth, you wondered what it would be like to have it on you. You told me you wanted to see my hair falling across my face as I called out your name. If you still want those things, Gabe, you can have them. You can have me. All you have to do is say you'll take on this negotiation."

"You're offering yourself to me, princess?" The carved planes of his face hardened. "Any way I like, any time or place?"

She felt herself flush. "That's the offer. Do you—"

She'd forgotten how fast Gabe Riggs could move when he wanted to. He was still holding the shotgun in his right hand, but the heavy cuff bracelet gleamed silver as he caught her two wrists together with his left, his grip tight.

"Still the lady of the manor, aren't you. And I'm still the hired hand, as far as you're concerned—the man you snap your fingers for when you've got a job, like standing at stud for you when you're bored with your usual escorts, or like bringing back your husband-to-be."

His face was so close to hers that she could see

tiny flecks of gold light up the dark amber of his eyes. She shook her head swiftly, and saw the amber turn to obsidian.

"It's not like that—"

"Damn straight it's not like that, honey," he said. "Yeah, there's been a time or two in the past eighteen months when I've thought of how you looked and tasted and sounded while I was going out of my mind and loving it that night. Hell, why wouldn't I remember? It's not like there's been another woman to replace those memories—not here in the middle of nowhere. But just because I've been living like a saint in the desert for a year and a half doesn't mean all you have to do is lean back against your car, give me a little glimpse of those satin thighs of yours, and I'll be so grateful for the chance to take you again that I'll promise you anything."

He released his grip on her wrists. Against the paleness of her skin the impression of his fingers remained.

"Let me tell you how it's going to be, princess," he said steadily. "I'm going to take on the job of getting Jess back safely, but for no other reason than that I've got a conscience. Not only could Kanin's grandstanding jeopardize the life of one of my oldest friends—" his tone took on a sudden harshness "—but it could put a child in danger. That's unacceptable."

Relief rushed through her, so sharp and intense that it felt like pain. Tears prickled at the back of her eyes and spilled over onto her lashes. "You'll take on the job? Oh, Gabe—"

"There's one more thing that's going to happen, honey," he went on. "One of these days you're going to come to me for the third time, except it won't be to bolster your ego or take on a hostage negotiation. It'll be because you remember, too."

He brought a tanned hand to her chin and tilted it upward so that she couldn't avoid his eyes. "I know you do, princess," he said in an edged whisper. "No matter what you said the morning after, you loved it just as much as I did, didn't you? So one day you're going to show up on my doorstep, and whatever reason you give for being there, I'm going to know what you want...and even if it takes every last ounce of self-control I have, I'm going to turn you down."

She'd been on a roller coaster of emotions for the past twenty-four hours, Caro thought, her gaze trapped by the coldness in his. Since receiving the call from Jess's kidnappers, she'd swung from fear to hope to despair, but what she was feeling right now wasn't any of those.

It was anger. And what made it worse was that it was mixed with a flicker of desire. She pushed his hand away.

"No, you're not," she said, her voice as icy as she could make it. "Because you also said that when you looked at me you saw heat that could sear a brand onto a man. You might try to deny it, but I think you let yourself be branded by me that night...and I think deep down you'd give anything to feel that brand burning into you again."

Just for an instant she saw bleak self-knowledge shadow the antagonism in his gaze, and knew that her barb had struck home. Pride prompted her to sink it in a little deeper.

"I won't even have to say please, will I, Gabe," she said coolly. "If the day ever comes that I want what you have to offer, I'll just show up and all that self-control of yours will disappear like it did once before."

Even as the unforgivable words left her mouth she wanted to call it back, but it was too late. The shotgun still at his side, one-handedly Gabe pulled her to him, his face so close to hers that his words were spoken against her lips.

"You just set the ground rules again. I don't think I've ever heard you say 'please' and mean it. One of these days you will."

Resisting the impulse to struggle free from his grasp, Caro met his eyes. "Is that a threat?"

"A threat?" He brought his mouth down one last fraction of an inch to hers. "Hell, no."

His kiss was immediately deep. Shock and anger lent an immediate edge to her response. Her hands flew to his chest to push him away.

Then slowly, her fingers curled into her palms, twin handfuls of Gabe's shirt clutched tightly in them.

For eighteen months she'd told herself she'd remembered it wrong, Caro thought light-headedly— that Gabriel Riggs's kiss couldn't have been like summer lightning racing through her, a shower of sparks sizzling along all her nerve endings at once. But she'd remembered it right. Except memory wasn't a substitute for the real thing.

And the real thing was impossible to resist.

Abruptly Gabe lifted his mouth from hers. As if they'd been doused with a bucket of ice water, the sparks and the summer lightning were instantly extinguished.

His eyes, so pale that for a moment they seemed lupine, blazed down at her expressionlessly. At the side of his neck a trip-hammer pulse gave the lie to his air of control.

"Not a threat, a promise." His smile held no humor at all. "And I'm going to be right there when you keep it, princess."

# Chapter Three

"Dammit, Caro, this Riggs character you've foisted on us has been hiding out in the desert for a year and a half. The man's obviously unstable, to say the least." Crawford Solutions' vice president Steve Dixon's balding head gleamed with sweat, despite the air-conditioning keeping the sticky heat of the Mexican evening outside at bay. "Right now, he's upstairs going through Jess's private papers and belongings instead of conferring with us. If that doesn't point to his incompetence, I don't know what does."

Dixon's objection was a variation of the same ones he'd made upon her and Gabe's arrival at Jess's Lazy J Ranch a few hours ago, Caro thought in frustration, when she'd informed him that Gabe was now the negotiator in charge of the case. He'd kept them up during the brief flight across the border to the Crawford Solutions' villa here in Mexico's Chihuahua Province, and he was still trying to persuade her to change her mind. The only difference was that now he had an ally.

With his cadre of paramilitary types milling around and a Recoveries International command post already established at the villa—in one corner of the room a technician was checking a bewildering array of wires and computer monitors hooked up to the telephone in preparation for the kidnappers' expected phone call— it was obvious Larry Kanin didn't intend to be replaced without a fight, as he now made clear.

"Living like a hermit didn't drive our boy Gabriel round the bend. Fouling up the last job he did for me before I fired him was what made him snap," Kanin drawled. "Like I told you, Steve, the man crashed a party at my Aspen chalet. I had to get physical with him before he would leave."

The Caroline Moore who'd been Larry's fiancée was a woman she didn't even know anymore, Caro thought. How had she ever contemplated marrying him? Nothing about him seemed quite real, from the crisp wave in his dark brown hair to his air of concern over Jess's abduction.

*At least I never slept with the man,* she told herself thankfully. *If I had, I don't think I could stand being in the same room as him. I just wish I hadn't had to make Gabe believe the relationship had gone that far.*

But then, she wished a lot of things when it came to Gabriel Riggs. Right at the top of that wish list was the futile desire that she'd come off a little better than she had in their confrontation earlier.

There were two people in the world against whom the shields she'd kept up all her life were useless. One of them was Emily, right now safely in the care of Mrs. Percy, a local woman who'd baby-sat her since her birth and who had agreed to spend tonight at the Lazy J. At the thought of her small daughter, Caro instinctively wrapped her arms around herself, as if in them she could feel the weight and warmth of a tiny body.

From the moment she'd first learned she had a new life growing inside her she'd willingly laid her heart bare to every piercing joy, every numbing fear, every emotion possible that came with the all-enveloping love she felt toward the baby she'd been blessed with. Emily was one of the two people who left her vulnerable, and that was as it should be between a mother and her child.

But Gabe Riggs was the other person she couldn't seem to shield herself against, and that wouldn't do at all.

She'd gone to him today determined not to let anything of what she'd felt for him in the past show in her face, her voice, her actions. But his coldness toward her had shattered all her protective barriers, and she'd struck out at him in the only way she knew how.

She'd been the ice princess he remembered her to be. And then she'd melted at his kiss the way he'd known she would. Without even trying, he'd smashed through her every defence.

Every defence except one, she thought shakily. She'd kept the facts of Emily's parentage to herself. To make sure she continued keeping that secret safe, she would have to build her defences higher and stronger where Gabriel Riggs was concerned…even if that meant she had to be the rich bitch he'd known her as eighteen months ago.

But her own deception didn't mean she had to

stand here and listen to Kanin's untruths. She flicked a dismissive glance Larry's way.

"The way I heard it, the only thing you got physical with was a bowl of salmon mousse. Plus Jinx, of course," she added. "But none of that matters. Jess gave me the power to make this kind of decision in his absence, and I've hired Gabe. It's up to him to decide whether he uses whatever resources you might put at his disposal."

"Me, working under Riggs?" Kanin's lips curled. "I don't see why I should loan my equipment and people to the man who's replacing me. Sorry, Steve, I have to draw the line somewhere."

"But see, Larry, this time everyone's going to know about the line you drew. And if that line means the difference between Jess Crawford coming home alive or not, you won't be able to sweep his death under the carpet the way you did Leo Roswell's."

Despite herself, Caro felt quick heat race through her as Gabe entered the room, his hands in the pockets of his khaki pants, blue-black hair brushing the collar of his faded shirt. His careless attire and attitude were in marked contrast to Dixon's business suit and sweating agitation and Kanin's silk roll-neck sweater, tailored pants and indignant frown.

With only the barest of nods to acknowledge her presence, he went on, his gaze on Kanin.

"My old pal Jess has a heftier bank account than Leo did, for one thing. For another, if anything happens to a billionaire software genius who's got friends in high places, heads are going to roll—yours included, Larry, if it gets out that you withheld help you could have given.''

In the face of a veiled threat like that, her ex-fiancé really hadn't had much of a choice, Caro admitted a few minutes later. In fact, with his well-honed ability to grab credit, within moments Larry had seemingly persuaded himself that cooperation had been his idea.

''The perp's phone call is due to come in at around nineteen-hundred hours,'' he said, jerking his head at the nearby Recoveries International technician.

Gabe nodded at the man. ''It's been a while since we worked together, Jackson. How've you been, buddy?''

''Not bad, Gabe.'' The technician's smile held genuine warmth. ''I'm ready to roll here.''

Gabe's grin was swift. ''Good man. Then, I'll just use the next half hour to familiarize myself with the players involved. I might as well start with you, Dixon.''

Steve looked affronted. ''Unless you think I had something to do with this, why waste time grilling me?''

''For the same reason I wanted to look around Jess's study when I arrived,'' Gabe told him. ''It helps to get the whole picture of an abductee—''

''I understand you knew Jess when the two of you were in some kind of reform school together,'' Kanin interjected smoothly. ''Not that I've ever done juvenile time myself, but wouldn't that mean you already know him pretty well?''

It was meant to be a pinprick, Caro realized. It was clear how Larry intended to work this—on the surface he would extend his company's resources and cooperation, just in case he was ever called to account for his part in the matter, but whenever he could, he intended to erode what little confidence Dixon and anyone else had in Gabe's capabilities.

And from the tightening of Gabe's jaw, he knew exactly what Kanin was trying to do.

"I was a sixteen-year-old car-thief and Jess was a smart-ass seventeen-year-old, expelled from school for hacking into the computer system and boosting his friends' grades. In the fifteen years since, we've both taken different paths. I need to know more about the man he is now."

As if he'd wasted all the time he intended to with Larry, he turned back to Dixon. "I understand you've been with Crawford Solutions since the start?"

"Jess was working out of his garage when we met at a trade show in my hometown of Detroit," the executive said impatiently. "When he asked me to join his team, I told him he had some moxy, expecting me to throw my lot in with his fly-by-night operation. He didn't take offense—well, if you know Jess you know he never does," he added with a reluctant grin.

Gabe had called Jess one of the good guys, Caro thought as Dixon continued telling Gabe how Jess's persuasiveness had convinced him to join Crawford Solutions. Beneath his corporate slickness, Steve Dixon's liking for his partner was equally sincere. And she herself owed Jess more than she could ever repay, with all he had done for her after her father disowned her.

She could barely remember the mother who'd died

so long ago in a car accident. But she'd grown up taking her father's indulgence for granted, had thought she could wrap him around her little finger. She hadn't realized he'd seen her solely as an appendage of himself.

It was funny, Caro reflected, giving only half her attention to Dixon's explanation to Gabe about how the company worked, including the fact that besides she and Steve, a handful of other key employees had their living quarters on the Lazy J Ranch. Eighteen months ago, the shallow, insecure woman she'd been had scuttled back as fast as she could to the familiar security of her father's status-conscious world because she hadn't wanted to admit that her night with Gabe had changed her in any way. Within weeks she'd been cast out of William Moore's world—and his life—herself.

Jess had offered her much more than just a paycheck and a home. Being Jess, he'd become her friend, with no strings attached. He'd never asked who the father of her baby was, although she assumed he privately thought it was Larry, and when Emily was born he treated her like a cherished niece. Even when he'd asked Caro to marry him he made it plain that if her answer was no, she wasn't to worry that it would cost her her job or his friendship.

Except, her answer wasn't going to be no, Caro thought. She'd come to that decision only hours ago, when she'd seen Gabriel Riggs again for the first time in a year and a half and had realized with numb certainty that she hadn't gotten over him at all.

*I can't ever let you know you have a daughter,* she

told him silently, her gaze taking in the slight frown on his hard features, the air of lazy alertness in his attitude as he put a question to Dixon and received an answer. *So I'm never going to be able to let you know that your daughter's mother has always wondered how things might have been if you hadn't already disappeared from the face of the earth when she tried to phone you to tell you she was pregnant.*

Because wondering was foolish. Gabe had no desire to settle down, while Jess was more than willing to. Providing Emily with a father who would be there for her took precedence over all else, Caro reminded herself.

"...aside from Andrew Scott, a kid I brought to Jess's attention who for a while was his latest protegé, that's everyone I can think of. But Scott left Crawford Solutions a week ago, so he's not in the picture anymore. Any other questions, Riggs?"

The edge in Steve Dixon's voice wrenched Caro from her thoughts, and almost thankfully she thrust her own problems to the back of her mind.

"Just one," Gabe replied. "You said Jess paid his employees more than they could make anywhere else. What reason did his protegé give for leaving?"

"Scott didn't leave of his own volition, Jess fired him. He was a genius, but he was also a typical computer nerd—couldn't get along with anyone, always had his back up over something." Steve grimaced. "I think he and Jess—"

Whatever else he'd been about to say was abruptly cut off by the ringing of the phone. Immediately Larry reacted, his voice sharp with tension.

"Put it on speaker." His command was directed to the technician.

Gabe countered the order instantly. "Not yet, Jackson. Give it two more rings." His manner was businesslike, but his voice betrayed a hint of warning as he went on. "My show, Larry, remember? Pick it up on the first ring and you've already handed the caller the advantage before a single word's spoken. Second ring, he still knows you were sitting there waiting for him. By the end of the third ring he's starting to get a little antsy."

The phone rang again.

"You can bet this isn't a cold call. He'll be working from a script, whether it's written down or not. Emotion's going to make him want to deviate from his script, and if he does he's more likely to make a slip."

"So what if he slips up?" Caro heard her own voice rise. "They've still got Jess. We're still going to do what they say, aren't we?"

The phone rang a third time. Gabe nodded, his eyes meeting hers for the first time since he'd walked into the room.

"Yeah, we're going to do what they say. But the more we know about them and how they react, the better, especially if anything goes wrong during the handover." He moved toward the phone. "And handovers never go exactly to plan, do they, Jackson."

"You got that right, Gabe," Kanin's man said tensely. "On your signal."

"Now."

Even as Gabe pressed the speaker button on the

phone, Caro heard a tiny *ping* as the fourth ring began and was cut off. Out of the corner of her eye she saw Jackson flick a switch on his equipment.

"Dixon? You there?"

At the kidnapper's abrupt question, Jackson glanced at his monitors. Her heart pounding, Caro gave her full attention to Gabe.

"Dixon's not handling this. My name's Riggs and I'm the hostage negotiator in charge. What do I call you?"

There was a pause. Then the caller spoke again, his tone oddly metallic.

"How about Leo, Riggs? Or does that name bring back bad memories?"

Caro was close enough to see the muscle that jumped at the side of Gabe's jaw as he answered. "You've made your point—you've heard of me but I don't know anything about you. Fair enough. I'm ready and willing to deal under whatever name you choose, but first I want to know for sure that Crawford's still alive. Put him on or I'm hanging up."

"No, dammit!" The shocked exclamation came from Dixon. Gabe nailed him with a glance and turned back to the phone.

"Put Jess on, Leo. The lady who's calling the shots has given me a free hand to deal the cards as I see fit, no matter what anyone else here might say. If I can't satisfy myself that the man I'm negotiating for is alive, all bets are off."

"Gabe? Hell, old buddy, so Caro found you, did she?"

The voice was weak and uneven, but unmistakably

Jess's, although the forced jauntiness in his tone was a pale facsimile of his normal good humor. Without warning Caro felt a sob catch in her throat.

"She found me." Gabe's smile was strained. "Jess, this is procedure, okay? I need proof that it's you. What was the name of that hammerheaded Appaloosa Del Hawkins had on the Double B when we were kids? The one with such a wicked temper none of us could ever ride it?"

Jess's laugh was shaky. "Chorizo," he said promptly. "He's still on the Double B. And dammit, you Navajo son of a gun, I happen to know that you rode the brute after Tye and Con and I gave up on him."

"Bravo, Riggs." The metallic voice was back on the line, and this time Caro thought she heard a touch of mockery beneath his words. "Bravo. You've proven you're a professional and not about to take my word for anything. Satisfied?"

"That it's Jess, and he's still alive? Yeah, I'm satisfied," Gabe said evenly. "What are your terms, Leo?"

"Five million in bearer bonds if we can finalize this within forty-eight hours. The price goes up considerably if you need more time."

"Two million and you get it tonight at a handover point of your choice." Gabe's reply was flat. "Take it, Leo. You know I won't be able to get the authorities involved in an ambush at such short notice, so it's a deal you shouldn't pass up."

"Three million."

The technician stiffened. Touching Gabe on the

arm, he nodded toward the screen in front of him and gave a thumbs-up. Following Gabe's gaze, Caro saw that the scrolling lines of numbers on Jackson's monitor had been replaced by a single ten-digit one, accompanied by a street address and the city location of Tijuana. Gabe nodded, started to switch his attention back to the phone, and stopped.

The scrolling numbers had reappeared. They were replaced again, this time by another number and a highlighted address in—

Caro stared at the monitor, confused. *Oshawa, Canada?* Surely that couldn't be right. She blinked as a third number and city came up on the screen.

Jackson slumped back in his chair, shaking his head in defeat.

Gabe kept his voice even. "Three million in bearer bonds. When and where?"

"In an hour, where the road takes a curve at the fifteen-mile mark from the villa," came the succinct answer. "And Riggs—just you, Dixon and the woman Crawford mentioned. She's his fiancée, I understand. Not that I think you're amateur enough to be considering a double cross of me and my people, but with a woman present, I know you won't take risks."

"You're damn right I won't risk the woman. She's not—" Gabe began, but the kidnapper cut him off.

"That part's nonnegotiable, negotiator. If she doesn't show, your friend Jess ends up the way Leo Roswell did."

Abruptly the line went dead.

Kanin's excited voice was the first to break the silence. "Did we find out where the bastard was calling from?"

Jackson shook his head in frustration. "He had some kind of scrambling device that was way beyond anything I've ever come up against before. And his voiceprint was fed through a filter."

"He's arrogant." Gabe flexed his shoulders, and Caro heard a tendon pop. "That's useful to know."

"He was taunting you, wasn't he?" she said, watching him closely. "That's why he chose the name Leo—to show you he knew what happened on your last case."

"Which doesn't mean squat," Kanin said loudly. "For God's sake, Rosten's death was front-page news at the time."

"*Roswell,* Larry. Leo Roswell." Gabe looked at Caro, his gaze holding nothing more than professional assessment. "Yeah, he was taunting me. But his attitude just might trip him up and lead to his capture."

"You really think that's possible?" Dixon's tone was eager. "Dammit, man, if you can somehow foil these bastards, Crawford Solutions'll owe you big time. The ransom's coming out of the company's own pockets, you know. Since Jess never used body-guards, the insurance companies refused to cover him for this kind of contingency. What are you planning?"

"I'm planning to hand over the three million in bearer bonds Caro informed me earlier today was on hand," Gabe said. "I'm planning to get Jess back home safely. I'm not planning to do anything—*any-*

*thing,* understand?—that could get him or anyone else killed.''

He rubbed his jaw, and again Caro glimpsed tension behind his gesture. ''Jess's abductors are going to be pissed off enough as it is when you and I show up alone, Dixon—but that can't be helped.''

''Leo said my presence at the handover was nonnegotiable,'' she interjected. ''If Jess's safe return hinges on my being there, I intend—''

''I don't give a damn about your intentions, you're not going,'' Gabe said. ''And *that's* nonnegotiable.''

''Then you're off this case.'' She held his gaze, hoping she was half as good as he was at concealing tenseness. ''I hired you, and if you force me to, I can fire you.''

His expression hardened. ''Like I said earlier, handovers never go according to plan. If one of those thugs gets spooked, all hell could break loose within a matter of seconds.''

''And me not showing up could be the very thing that spooks them,'' Caro countered. ''I mean it, Gabe. I go along on the handover or you're off the negotiation. I owe Jess that much.''

''No offense, Riggs, but I can't say I'm sorry Caro's finally seen the light.'' Dixon turned to Kanin. ''You've got, what, Larry—ten men available? Couldn't we wait until they spring Jess and then surround the scumbags?''

Kanin nodded judiciously. ''I think it's—''

''You win.''

Ignoring everyone else, Gabe covered the few feet between him and Caro with a stride. She looked up into his face as his grip bit into her shoulders, and felt a moment's apprehension at the spark of anger in his gaze.

"But you knew you would, didn't you, princess," he said, his tone pitched for her ears only. "From the moment we first met you've counted on always getting what you want from me—whether it's a ride to Aspen, one last hostage negotiating job, or going against my instincts and taking you along on a handover."

His smile was tight. "You should know that I've got a limit where you're concerned, Caro. Do you get me, princess?"

He was so close to her that as he spoke the warmth of his breath touched the corners of Caro's lips. The apprehension she'd been feeling was cancelled out by another emotion.

Gabe Riggs didn't answer to any man anymore, she realized shakily. Where once his power had seemed kept on a firm leash, sometime during his self-imposed isolation that leash had been gnawed through and discarded forever.

He was more dangerous than she'd thought. And she was less able to resist his dangerous appeal than she'd so rashly promised herself she would be.

She felt herself sway an infinitesimal distance toward him. The air around them seemed suddenly heavy. Slow heat suffused her and she felt the warmth of faint color touch her cheeks.

"I get you, Gabriel," she said, her tone as barely audible as his had been. "But how am I going to know when you've reached that limit?"

The amber eyes watching her blinked. The hard grip on her shoulders slid fractionally down her arms and then stopped. Today when she'd confronted him under the merciless desert sun, the man hadn't seemed to notice the temperature or to be bothered by her unexpected appearance, she thought—but Gabe Riggs was bothered now.

And she could tell by just looking at him that he was feeling the same sudden heat that she was.

He released her.

''You won't. You'll just know when you've pushed me past it,'' he said tonelessly. He turned away, his jaw rigid.

''The clock's ticking, princess. Let's go save the man you're going to marry.''

## Chapter Four

"What time is it?"

Steve had asked that same question twice already in the past half hour, Caro thought edgily, but Gabe, beside her in the driver's seat of the stationary sports utility, betrayed no impatience at having to answer him yet again. He glanced at his watch, pressing a button on the side of its dial as he did.

"Ten-thirty." The faint phosphorescence that had momentarily lit up the watch face faded. He switched his attention back to the blackness of the night. "Yeah, they were supposed to show up half an hour ago, Dixon, but don't start imagining the worst. From my reading of Leo's character, I'd guess he's making us wait on purpose."

"To prove he's the one calling the shots in this situation?" From the back seat Steve gave an angry snort. "I've got news for you, Riggs. He is, dammit. The bastard's got us all dancing to his tune, and I for one don't like it. Larry thinks Leo and his gang are probably no more than street punks who saw a chance to snatch a careless *Americano* businessman, and I don't mind telling you, it galls me that someone in my position should have to knuckle under to nobodies like that."

Caro had heard enough. She twisted around to face the Crawford Solutions vice president. "So what do you propose, Steve? That we drive off just to prove your point? Nobodies or not, these thugs have Jess, and until he's out of danger I'd say that gives them every right to call whatever shots they want." Her voice shook on the final few words and swiftly she faced forward in her seat again, fighting to keep her ragged emotions under control.

She felt rather than saw Gabe direct a glance her way before he spoke, his tone brooking no argument. "The lady's right, Dixon. If Jess's kidnappers want to play a few head games with us before they release him, we let them. Abductions are never just about the money, they're about control—who's got it, who wants it, and who's willing to relinquish it."

"Then, why did you baulk at paying the price Leo asked?" Steve asked. "Not that I don't appreciate you getting the final sum down a couple million, but with Jess such a pal of yours it seems more than a little callous of you to have haggled so closely over his ransom, Riggs."

Steve could be pompous at times, Caro told herself, and he had a keen eye for the bottom line that had sometimes placed him at odds with his easier-going boss, but a cut like the one he'd just delivered was more Larry's style than his own. She had the sudden conviction that while she and Gabe had been collecting the suitcase of bearer bonds from the villa's safe before leaving for this rendezvous with Jess's abductors, Larry had seized the opportunity to further erode Dixon's confidence in Gabe. From Gabe's closed expression it appeared he'd come to the same conclusion.

"Two points, Dixon," he said tersely, his gaze fixed on the empty road ahead. "One, my job description reads 'hostage negotiator.' I negotiated with Leo over the price because if I hadn't he would have figured he'd asked for too little in the first place, and that might have convinced him that handing a valuable hostage over so easily would be a mistake. I said it was about control. I didn't say it was about rolling over to a kidnapper's every demand."

"Like I said, I'm not complaining—" Dixon muttered, but Gabe went on before he could finish.

"My second point is this—Kanin's dead wrong about these people being no more than street thugs. Street thugs wouldn't have the kind of sophisticated scrambling devices that bypassed Jackson's tracing equipment, or the filter that made it impossible to get an identifiable print from Leo's voice."

"So you're saying Jess's situation is even worse than it could be," Dixon said, the bluster draining from his tone. "Punks lucking into a big score would be preferable to a well-organized group of professionals who've covered all the bases."

"Hell, no." Gabe's reply was swift. "Professionals can be counted on not to let their emotions get in the way of doing business. It's the amateurs and cowboys who make me nerv—"

He stopped in midsentence. Dixon started to say something, but Gabe's uplifted palm silenced him.

Try as she might, she couldn't hear or see what had alerted the big man beside her, as in vain she focused her vision on the dark road. But she had no doubt that his sudden tenseness was justified. During the hours she'd been with Gabriel Riggs today she'd realized that his sojourn in the desert had sharpened senses already well-honed, as evidenced by his instantaneous reaction to the threat of the rattler.

Her senses had been heightened, too, she thought, although not in any way that was proving useful. The opposite, in fact. Even at a time like this, all she seemed to be able to concentrate on was Gabe's nearness, his tone of voice, his slightest move.

*For heaven's sake, you're actually inhaling the scent of the man. It's just plain soap and water, but you're breathing it in as if it's pure oxygen and you can't get enough of it,* she told herself in frustration.

Which was stupid—no, more than stupid, irresponsible. They were here to save the man she'd decided to marry. She should be concentrating on Jess and the matter at hand.

Except, she didn't want to—no more than Dixon, with his needling and his nervous checking of the time, wanted to concentrate on the reason why they were waiting by the side of a pitch-dark road in the middle of nowhere. If everything went as planned, within moments they would be face-to-face with the mysterious Leo and his crew. Professionals or not, Jess's kidnappers were cold-blooded enough to have put a price on a man's life, and as Gabe had warned on the drive here, one wrong move during the handover could not only sign their hostage's death warrant but place everyone's life in jeopardy.

*He was right not to want me to come.* A wave of apprehension washed over her. *I shouldn't be here. No matter what I owe Jess, my first priority should have been Emily. As her mother, I never should have put myself in a situation like—*

"That little daughter of yours," Gabe said without looking at her. "What did you say her name was?"

Even as he spoke Caro heard the faint rumble of what sounded like a vehicle approaching, although the bend in the road in front of the sports utility meant the only visible indication was a slight lessening of the blackness, as if faraway headlights were cutting through the night. She smoothed damp palms on the linen slacks she'd changed into earlier.

"Emily," she replied tensely. "Why?"

He ignored the question, his gaze, like hers, fixed on the telltale brightness chasing away more of the shadows ahead of them. "Emily," he repeated, his tone too low to be heard by Dixon in the back seat. "Okay, so when you get back home tonight and look in on Emily, whether she's sleeping or not, you tell her Gabe Riggs made her a vow tonight. You tell her I promised her nothing was going to happen to her mule-headed mother during this handover. You think you can remember to do that?"

A moment ago the last thing she'd have thought herself capable of was laughter. A surprised little hiccup escaped her. Caro cast a grateful look at his expressionless profile.

"I'll remember," she said unevenly. "And Gabe—

I'm sorry I fought you on this. I hired you because of your expertise in this kind of thing, and then I went over your head and insisted on coming along. You've got every right to be mad at me.''

''More than just mad, dammit,'' he muttered out of the corner of his mouth. ''I figure I've got every right to want to tan that sweet backside of yours when we get back to the Lazy J, but I suppose if I tried, you'd crack me a good one across the chops like you did once before, right?''

Just for a moment he glanced sideways toward her, and suddenly Caro found her shakiness had absolutely nothing to do with the approaching headlights.

Maybe if she hadn't had him, she told herself faintly, taking in the hard line of his jaw, the coppery gleam of his tanned skin in the glow of the instrument panel, the wry lift at the corner of his lips. Maybe if she had no idea what she was missing, she wouldn't feel this insane *hunger* for the man. Or maybe it wouldn't make any difference at all to the way she felt when she looked at him.

*Hunger* was a good word for what she was feeling. So was *heat.* So was *weakness,* and weakly she gave in to a reckless impulse.

''I don't know,'' she said, meeting his gaze directly. ''I can think of certain circumstances where I just might indulge you in that particular little fantasy, Gabe.''

Even with the inadequate illumination she saw his eyes briefly widen and then narrow at her.

''I wish you didn't like playing with fire so much,

princess," he said softly. "Especially since everytime you do, I'm the one who ends up getting burned."

He switched his attention back to the road, and although there was no more space between them than there had been a second ago, with the abrupt action he seemed to distance himself from her. He frowned at the now brilliant swaths of light cutting through the darkness.

"Do me a favor?" he asked curtly.

If the recklessness that had possessed her hadn't already ebbed away and been replaced by cold sanity, Caro thought, his attitude would have doused it. She swallowed and nodded. "Of course," she managed to say, hoping her own voice sounded as detached as his. "What do you need me to do?"

"When we get your fiancé back, insist on a fast wedding and don't bother inviting me, no matter what my old buddy Jess says." He lifted his shoulders in a shrug, still without taking his attention from the road. "Somehow I don't think I can totally trust myself not to give in to the urge to play with fire, too, where you're concerned. And like I said, someone's bound to get burned."

Even if she'd been able to muster a reply, she didn't get the chance. Her lips still parted in disconcertion at his admission, she saw twin headlights rounding the bend in the road up ahead and blaze blindingly toward them. Instinctively she turned away, shielding her eyes from the sudden glare, and noticed Dixon's arm come up in a similarly startled gesture.

Gabe's reaction was the only one that brought results. Unhurriedly he reached toward the instrument panel and turned on the SUV's high-beams. As soon as he did, the approaching vehicle dimmed its own.

"We went over everything on the drive here, so you both know what's expected," he said calmly. "Dixon, take your cues from me, not the kidnappers. Caro, you stay near the car unless I specifically tell you different. And if anything happens to me, I want the two of you to get the hell out of here and away from these bastards by whatever means possible, understood?"

"Understood," Dixon said quickly. "But what if—"

"There aren't any what-if's," Gabe overrode him, reaching for the door handle as the other vehicle came to a stop at an angle in front of them, effectively blocking the road. "I go down, you two leave me here. That's an order."

He'd done this dozens of times before, Caro thought, fumblingly unlatching her own door and pushing it open, but this situation was as alien to her as if she'd suddenly been dropped into the middle of a bad movie. She stepped out of the car, the sticky night air wrapping around her like an extra skin and her sleeveless cotton blouse already wilting against her body, although the loose-fitting white shirt Gabe was wearing didn't seem to be sticking to him.

A bad black-and-white movie, she qualified nervously as she took in the scene in front of her. Although the kidnappers' vehicle—some kind of boxy delivery-type truck, she realized, and so readily identifiable by the name on its side, Dos Abejas Fruit

Company, that it had to be stolen—no longer had its high-beams on, its headlights created a two-dimensional aspect to everything. The heavy rumbling of the idling motor provided a soundtrack to the transaction about to take place.

Within a few minutes a man's life would be bartered for money. As horrible as such a concept was, that would be the best-case scenario. In a worst-case scenario, Jess would be—

There wasn't going to be a worst-case scenario, Caro told herself, shutting her mind to the nightmarish images her thoughts had conjured up. Gabe was a professional. Except for the negotiation that Larry Kanin's meddling had tragically derailed, he'd never yet failed to bring a hostage safely back. Jess had chosen well when he'd insisted that in such a situation he wanted his old friend handling his release.

"You are Riggs?"

The man who alighted from the passenger side of the truck was barrel-chested and dressed in rough, working-man's attire. Even factoring in the filter that had distorted Leo's conversation, he sounded nothing like the voice on the telephone. He had a strong accent, and instead of the arrogance that had been in Leo's tone, there was a hair-trigger edge to his question.

"Gabriel Riggs," Gabe confirmed, walking to within a few feet of his interrogator. He raised his voice enough to be heard over the truck's motor. "Where's the man who calls himself Leo? I thought I would be dealing with him."

His counterpart stepped fully into the light, and

Caro's breath caught in her throat. He was an older man, about fifty or so, and the leathery skin of his face seemed to be a road map of all the dark alleys and shadowed hiding places he'd seen in those brutal fifty years. A knife scar ran from the corner of one eye to his mouth, pulling his cheek downward. He grinned, and the scar turned his grin into a grimace.

"Sorry, my friend. Leo, he arrange the job, phone you an' everything, but he don't come to the handover. He send me and my men, tell us what he want us to do."

He shrugged, and without looking at the truck behind him, raised one fist and knocked twice on the vehicle's panel side. The knock was seemingly a signal, because Caro heard the metal *clang* of a latch being released from inside the truck, and slowly the panel began to slide sideways.

"I hope Riggs is keeping an eye on the joker behind the wheel."

Dixon's nervous whisper beside her ear made her jump, and it was all she could do not to turn furiously on him. "Gabe knows what he's doing, and if you and I are aware of the driver, I'm sure he is, too." She barely moved her lips as she spoke—mainly because they felt too numb with fear to move properly. "Don't worry about his end of things, worry about your own. Any minute now you're going to have to step forward with that briefcase and open it up for their inspection. They're going to want to check that the whole three million's there before they release Jess."

"Not that it's going to do the bastards any good."

At the odd note of satisfaction in Dixon's tone she looked at him, and his scowl instantly rearranged itself into a smile.

"I just mean that the authorities are bound to hunt them down sooner or later," he said quickly. "I don't imagine the *federales* are going to use kid gloves when they catch up to—dear God!"

For a moment Caro didn't understand what was behind his shocked exclamation, but then she looked past the fully opened side panel of the truck and the three rifle-toting men jumping from it to take their places by the scarred man. She felt the blood drain from her face as she saw what had prompted Dixon's horrified words.

The SUV's headlights flooded the interior of the truck. Dead center, as if pinned by a spotlight on a stage, was a man sitting on a wooden chair—no, not sitting, she thought faintly, but bound hand and foot to it by lengths of grease-stained rope. Two similarly stained rags served as a blindfold and a gag, but even the obscuring cloth couldn't conceal the raw and bleeding gashes on his cheek and temple, the latter wound half hidden by a thick strand of chestnut hair.

*Darn it, Jess, I told you to get a haircut before your business trip.* The foolish thought popped unbidden into her mind even as the bile rose in her throat. *And I distinctly remember saying that it wouldn't hurt to take a suit and a decent pair of shoes for once, instead of those disreputable high-tops and that garish Hawaiian shirt you seem to think is acceptable garb for meetings—*

"What the hell have you done to him?"

Gabe's voice was a whiplash. The flimsy defenses Caro's psyche had tried to erect came crashing down and the full horror of what she was looking at came rushing in on her. This was *Jess,* she thought sickly—a good man, a decent man, a man who was a sucker for stray dogs and lame ducks. He stuck by his friends. He made new ones at the drop of a hat. He told excruciatingly bad jokes and always forgot to tie his laces and could eat a whole carton of strawberry ice cream at one sitting.

None of that mattered to his abductors. They didn't even see him as a person. They'd used him as a punching bag, had trussed him up with cruelly tight knots, and—her blurred vision caught the fugitive gleam of light on metal and she saw a fourth gunman, pistol at the ready, standing farther back in the shadowed interior of the truck—they were prepared to execute him if they didn't get what they wanted. She felt hot tears spilling down her cheeks, and sank her teeth into her bottom lip.

''We had to slap him around a little, that's all.'' The speaker was one of the rifle-toting men, younger than his companions and with a razor-thin strip of beard bisecting his chin. He laughed, gesturing with his weapon toward Gabe. ''Hey, *compadre,* you don't look like no snowball to me. What do you care what happens to a rich gringo like this anyway? He get the chance, he put the damn boot on your neck—and you know it, man.''

''*Basta, tonto!*'' The scarred man rounded on the speaker, and although Caro would have sworn he carried no weapon on his person, with shock she saw he was holding a massive revolver to the younger man's head.

"Yes, I call you a fool," he said as his opponent stiffened. "Only a fool would wave his gun around so he can't use it when he needs it. And only a fool would forget who is supposed to be doing the talking here. The next time you open your mouth, I shut you up for good, understand?"

There was something badly wrong here, Caro thought apprehensively. She saw a slight frown cross Gabe's features and knew he was thinking the same. He'd based his assessment of the kidnappers on the sophistication of the mysterious Leo's equipment and manner, but these men weren't acting professionally at all.

*"It's the amateurs and cowboys who make me nervous…"* His earlier comment to Dixon came back to her, and her worry grew. Leo's crew weren't like him. They were a cutthroat band of thugs and criminals without any real organization, and as Gabe had said, that made them unpredictably dangerous. The scarred man was the only one who seemed to have any control of the situation, but for how long?

*"Jefe—"*

Gabe inclined his head at the scarred man, giving no attention at all to the others. Caro understood his tactic, both of dismissing the hired gunmen and of calling his opponent "leader." He was attempting to bring some semblance of order to the proceedings.

*"Jefe*, we have the bearer bonds as arranged. I will ask the representative of Crawford Solutions to place the briefcase in front of you."

There was a formality to his speech, and that, she guessed, was also deliberately assumed to defuse the emotions that had nearly boiled over a moment ago. It worked. The scarred man took a breath and nodded.

''The fat businessman, yes?''

Caro saw Dixon frown beside her at this slighting reference to his portliness, and gave a silent prayer of thanks when he remained prudently silent.

''Tell the *chica* to come forward, too.''

Gabe shook his head, still with the same air of calm. Lowering his voice, he said something in rapid Spanish, and was met with a sharp answer in the same language, accompanied by a scowl on the knife-gullied face. Again he shook his head, this time less calmly.

Whatever rapport he'd created with the leader of the crew was swiftly disintegrating, Caro realized. And it was her fault. She'd insisted on coming, but with Leo not here, it was likely her absence wouldn't have caused as much of a problem as Gabe's refusal now to bring her forward. There was only one solution.

Dixon had already moved to Gabe's side, briefcase in hand. Her legs feeling suddenly like rubber, she crossed in front of the SUV and took her place beside the Crawford Solutions' vice president.

A muscle jumped in Gabe's jaw. ''Get back by the car.''

She stood her ground, her gaze taking in Jess and the gunman guarding him. ''I came here to help, Gabe. Making these people angry isn't the way to go about that.''

"The woman has better sense than you, Mr. Riggs," the scarred man grunted. "You with the *cartera*—place it on the ground and open it."

His order was directed at Dixon. With a tightening of his lips Gabe looked away from Caro and nodded at the vice president.

"Go ahead and do what the man says, Dixon."

"Open the briefcase? Sure, Riggs."

Again Caro thought she detected an odd note in Dixon's tone, and despite his ready agreement he hesitated for a moment before setting the case on the ground and thumbing the latches. He flipped it open and took a step backward.

She was close enough to him to see his glance dart quickly past the SUV to the road behind them, as if fearful their transaction would be interrupted by a chance vehicle rounding the bend. But that was so unlikely as to be impossible. The road back led only to the villa, and although when Jess was in residence some of his household staff used it to come and go daily to their homes in the village a few miles ahead, right now only Larry and his men were—

A terrible suspicion suddenly filled Caro. Before her heart had a chance to take its next beat, suspicion solidified to icy certainty at the throaty rumble of a coasting vehicle's motor roaring to life as it swung around the final hilly curve from the villa and raced up the road behind them. A split-second later, blinding headlights blazed across the distance between Larry Kanin's approaching Hummer and the stationary SUV.

"*Emboscada?*" The scarred man's face twisted in

fury as he spat the word at Gabe. "You set up an ambush, *negociar? Madre de Dios,* you will pay for this insanity! All of you will pay—"

"Riggs had nothing to do with it, buddy," Dixon said with triumphant bravado. "Me and Larry Kanin screwed up your dirty little scheme, and in about ten seconds you and your punks are going to be surrounded by trained Recoveries International shooters. Tell your man in the truck to untie Jess and—"

"Shut the hell up, Dixon," Gabe snapped. He turned to the scarred man, raising his hands in a conciliatory gesture. "*Jefe,* take the bonds and go. When you get to a safe place, reassure yourself that the ransom's all there and then release Crawford. I'll wait for your phone call telling me where—"

"Forget it, negotiator." The snarled rejoinder came from the younger man, and in one fluid motion he brought his rifle up, aiming it straight at Caro. "You double-crossed us. You're going to see your woman die."

"I don't think so, *gamberro.*"

Gabe's hands were already at shoulder height. Even as the gunman's trigger finger started to move, with blurred speed he reached behind him to the back-holstered sawed-off shotgun concealed under his loose cotton shirt, pulled it up and over his shoulder, and fired it one-handed.

The blast caught the man full in the chest, driving him back with such force that he slammed against the body of the truck, his own weapon discharging as he fell. At the same time Caro felt herself falling, and for a confused moment thought she'd been hit. Then she saw the flash of silver on Gabe's wrist as he clamped his left hand to his opposite biceps.

He'd pushed her down and taken the bullet meant for her, she realized numbly as she scrambled to her feet. He'd deliberately put himself between her and—

"Get out of the line of fire!" The hoarse command had barely left his lips before he swung the shotgun toward a second gunman who was aiming at a seemingly frozen Steve Dixon. Caro saw the spasm of effort that crossed Gabe's carved features as he jacked another round into the shotgun's chamber and pulled the trigger before the man had a chance to take Dixon down.

The briefcase under his arm, the scarred man had reached the cab of the truck where the driver was already gunning the motor. As the third gunman threw his weapon into the back of the truck and hoisted himself up, Caro ran to Gabe's side.

"You're hurt!" Her eyes widened as she took in the extent of the blood soaking his once-white shirt.

He rounded grimly on her. "I told you to get out of the line of fire, princess. Now *go!*"

"But—"

Her protest died in her throat. She'd assumed he'd meant out of the line of *his* fire, Caro thought. He hadn't meant that at all.

Gravel spraying around it like water from a fountain, the Hummer braked only yards from the SUV. Before it had come to a complete stop, black-clad men began piling out, automatic weapons at the ready. One of them, his face smeared with greasy

camouflage stripes but the crisp curl in his hair a clue
to his identity, climbed onto the vehicle's hood.

''Commence fir—''

''Dammit, Kanin, don't give the order!'' Gabe
shouted the words over his shoulder as he spun Caro
around and propelled her in the direction of the road-
way's verge.

She felt his hand leave her, and she glanced back
to see him sprinting toward the truck as it began moving.

''You've got civilians here, for God's sake, and I
need to get Jess—''

Even as he reached the open panel door of the vehicle and started to pull himself onto its platform, the
night exploded as Kanin's men opened fire. In horror,
Caro saw the sudden scarlet blotch that appeared on
Gabe's khaki pant leg, saw him lose his grip and fall
to the ground, saw the truck's right rear tire coming
straight at him.

''Gabe, *move!*''

The scream was torn from her throat, but as she
began running toward him she saw him rolling out of
the way of the moving vehicle. She followed his agonized gaze to Jess's trussed-up figure and the man
guarding him, just as the shooter raised the automatic
in his hand and fired it point-blank into Jess Crawford's temple.

## Chapter Five

"I didn't mean for it to turn out this way. They weren't supposed to kill Jess, they were supposed to surrender, for God's sake!"

Steve Dixon's litany was getting tired, Caro thought in numb detachment. She'd had to listen to it on the drive back to the villa, hadn't been able to shut it out while she'd waited for the word on Gabe's condition from the Recoveries International medic who'd extracted the bullet from his shoulder and tended to the flesh wound on his leg, and had endured it throughout the flight on the Crawford Solutions' jet back to New Mexico and the Lazy J.

Only when she'd closeted herself in Emily's nursery upon arrival at the ranch had she escaped his barrage of justifications, but after breaking the news of Jess's death to a shaken Mrs. Percy and telling the grandmotherly baby-sitter what Caro needed her to do, unwillingly she'd made herself seek out Dixon to inform him of what she'd decided.

Steve would need to know where to contact her. She owed it to Jess—at the thought, tears filled her eyes again—not to allow the company he'd created to go into free fall over the coming weeks. The powers of attorney he'd recently signed effectively bound her and Dixon together to keep Crawford Solutions operating for the foreseeable future, at least.

"It doesn't matter how you thought it would turn out, Steve," she said tonelessly. "What matters is that Gabe warned you and Larry how dangerous it would be to interfere in this handover, and the two of you didn't listen to him. Because of your greed and Larry's recklessness, Jess is dead, Gabe came so close to being killed that he won't be fit to travel back from Mexico for a few days, and my daughter's life is in jeopardy."

"Emily?" Confusion drove the self-pity from Steve's voice. "How does she come into this?"

She gave him a disbelieving stare. "Have you forgotten what Leo threatened in his first phone call— that if anything went wrong, he'd come after me and my daughter?"

With some of his normal bluffness he waved his hand. "Kanin never took that threat seriously, and I—"

"Larry didn't take it seriously?" Even to her own ears her voice sounded thin. "That's supposed to reassure me?"

Anger flashed through her pain. "Listen to me, Steve, and listen good. I'm going to keep Emily safe, no matter what. And if either you or Larry Kanin interfere in any way at all with my plans, I'll make you sorry you were ever *born,* do you understand?"

"Hey, sweetie, it's me. Your ol' pal Steve, remember?" He fixed a placating expression on his features.

"No one's going to stop you from taking precautions. You want to hire extra Recoveries International guards to post around the perimeter of the Lazy J, we'll do it. I know you blame Larry for what happened tonight, but when you calm down—"

What little was left of her precarious self-control fled. "We saw a man murdered a few hours ago—a man we both cared for, a man who'd been a good friend to both of us! Why should I be calm, and who else should I blame besides you and Kanin?"

"Riggs fired the first shot, dammit," Dixon said with peevish defensiveness. "Larry says if he'd kept his cool—"

"He fired the first shot to take down a killer who was about to kill *me,*" Caro corrected him sharply. "By then, Larry's actions had left him no option."

She stepped away from him. "But if you can pin this on Gabe, your hands are clean, aren't they. I'm wasting my time, and this wasn't what I came to talk to you about anyway. I'm leaving the Lazy J tonight, Steve. I'm taking Emily to—"

"Forget it, princess. You and Emily are staying here, where I can be sure you're safe."

The growl coming from the open doorway was huskier than normal, but there was no mistaking it. Caro whirled to see Gabe, his shoulder bandaged and the bullet-proof vest he was wearing obviously on loan from one of Kanin's men.

Dizzying relief swept through her. No matter that she'd been told by the Recoveries International medic who'd attended him that despite his lapses into unconsciousness during the trip back to the villa Gabe's injuries weren't life-threatening, she'd still argued against returning to the Lazy J without him. Only her fears for her daughter's safety had finally persuaded her to accompany Dixon on the hasty departure from Mexico that Larry had advised him to make.

"I thought you were—" she began tremulously, but he cut her off.

"Out for the count?" He shook his head. "Not this Navajo. When I came to, I gulped down a couple of pain pills for my shoulder and persuaded Kanin's helicopter pilot to get me back over the border."

"Where's Larry?" Dixon frowned. "For God's sake, man, you didn't leave him stranded there, did you?"

Gabe spared him a glance. "To explain away the two dead bodies on the road, you mean? Straight up I did. But knowing him the way I do, I made sure I got my explanation in first, during a phone call I made before I left the villa to an old *compadre* of mine, Captain Ronrico Estavez of the *federales*. I told him exactly how everything had gone down tonight and said if he needed me to return to Mexico to give official testimony, I'd be glad to as soon as Leo was put out of commission."

The smile he directed at Steve was sharklike. "I saw flashing lights pull up to the villa as my 'coptor lifted off. I'd say Kanin's doing some fast talking just about now."

Beneath his almost flippant manner he was barely holding his anger back, Caro realized, taking in his tense stance, the way his hands hung at his sides, fingers slightly curled as if readying to become fists.

Steve could apparently read the ominous signals, as well as she could, because with a muttered imprecation he turned on his heel and left the room.

His departure had the flavor of a hasty retreat. She would have given almost anything to have been able to follow him, rather than stay here and stage her own confrontation with Gabe, but she didn't have that option.

"When you told your Mexican police friend you wanted to see Leo put out of commission, you meant you intended to go hunting for him yourself, didn't you." She saw by the tightening of his jaw that she'd surmised correctly, and went on in a stronger voice. "Which means that you're going to leave me and Emily here with hired protection guarding us. That's not good enough, Gabe."

"The men I have in mind are the best. Some of them are ex-Recoveries International operatives who quit the company after Kanin bought it a couple of years ago. The others are a mixed bag—one's a former Navy SEAL who worked with me on a job once and whom I'd trust with my life, another's a female cop who was undercover for years and who's as tough as they come. You and your daughter will be in good hands."

A shutter came down behind his gaze. "I owe it to Jess to track down the bastard who orchestrated his kidnapping and murder," he said curtly, turning away from her. "I failed an old friend tonight. I won't fail him again."

"Failed?" Frowning, she spoke to his back. "That's not how I see it. You put your life on the line—not just for Jess, but for me. No one man could have done more than—''

''You don't get it, do you.'' He faced her again, so abruptly that she took half a step backward. ''You think that if Dixon and Kanin hadn't interfered tonight, right now I'd be knocking back a couple of cold ones with my buddy Crawford and telling him that saving his hide was all in a day's work for me. You think I'd be glad I'd been there for an old Double B pal, right?''

''I don't think that, I know that,'' Caro said in confusion. ''For heaven's sake, what's this about, Gabe?''

''It's about maybe deep down some part of me saw Jess's death as a reprieve, princess,'' he said harshly. ''It's about me not feeling the sense of loss I should have when I saw him killed. All I could think was that now I wasn't ever going to hear that you'd become Mrs. Jess Crawford.''

The corners of his mouth lifted as he took in her frozen reaction. ''Hell of a note, isn't it? On one side of the scales I had a friend who would have gone to the wall for me. On the other was a woman I'd spent a single night with, a woman I didn't even particularly like. And it was no contest, honey—when you showed up at that gas station this morning and told me he'd asked you to marry him, just for a minute I saw Jess as the enemy.''

She had thought she'd changed, Caro told herself. It seemed she hadn't—or at least, not as much as she'd thought. Because out of everything the man in front of her had said, the self-absorbed woman she'd once been seized on the least important component.

Seized on it, examined it and found that it had the power to hurt her more than she would have imagined.

"A woman you don't particularly like?" Repeating his words had the same effect as turning a knife in a wound. She gave a brittle laugh. "Then, you're correct, I don't get it at all. You don't like me. You told me earlier today that if I ever wanted you again you'd turn down the opportunity to have me. I don't for a moment believe you were in any way responsible for Jess's murder, but if you were, I don't think finding Leo's going to make it right for you. I don't think anything ever will. So how can you stand there and tell me it was no contest?"

"Because even if the price was my soul, I'd sell it in a heartbeat and think you were worth damnation, sweetheart," he said tightly. "There's no good reason for me to feel that way, and I wish to hell I didn't, but I do. That's why I need to do the only right thing left for me, and hunt Leo down."

This time when he turned away from her there was an implacability about his posture that told Caro he'd said all he intended to on the subject. She supposed she had, too, she thought shakily.

His revelation hadn't changed anything. The man had confessed to an obsession with her, an obsession he wished he could reason away. He hadn't talked about a future between them. And that was a good thing, she told herself resolutely.

She needed to keep her distance from him, and by

his own admission there was a gulf as wide as a New Mexico canyon yawning between them. Now the only threat he posed to Emily's security was his insistence on hiring bodyguards to keep them safe here on the Lazy J—and that wasn't his call, it was hers.

Hers and Jess's.

"I'm sure the people you have in mind are good, but they'd still be hired protection." She turned toward the door, pausing only to look back at him. "And you're wrong. Hunting Leo down is the easy thing for you to do, not the right thing. The right thing would be to follow Jess's last wishes, but you gave me your answer on that before you even knew he'd been kidnapped."

"What the hell are you talking about?" He glanced over his shoulder at her, lines of pain and exhaustion suddenly apparent in his face as their gazes met.

She shrugged. "Double B band-of-brothers reunion? Thanks but no thanks? I think that's how you put it. Come to think of it, you never did tell me why Jess's memories of Del Hawkins and his boot camp for wayward teens were so different from yours. Why your attitude toward the place and the man didn't jibe with anyone else's, for that matter."

"'Anyone else' being Tyler Adams and Virgil Connor?" Gabe frowned. "Lady, I'm damned if I know what my reckless youth has to do with anything, but I'll play along if that's what you want. Like I told Kanin this afternoon, I was a sixteen-year-old car thief who was given the choice between the Double B or real time. I chose the Double B, figuring a year at a ranch run by a Vietnam vet who needed a wheelchair to get around was better than jail. If I had to do it all over again, I'd take the lockup, believe me.''

His smile was tight. ''Former Marine Lieutenant Hawkins made my life hell for that year. I did my best to return the favor. When I finally shook the dust of the Double B from my boots, I vowed I'd never see it or that leatherneck son of a bitch again, and only Jess was ever fool enough to try to change my mind.''

A different kind of pain crossed his features before the shutters came down behind his eyes again. He shook his head. ''I don't know how many times over the years he asked me along when he paid Del a visit. Never say die, that was our Jess.''

''Yes, that was Jess,'' Caro agreed past the lump in her throat. She met his gaze, and at the sight of the telltale brilliance lighting the amber eyes she felt tears come to her own again. ''He still hasn't given up, Gabe. Are you going to turn him down this final time, too?''

''What do you mean?''

''I mean, Jess made me promise him two things a few weeks ago. The first was that if he was kidnapped, I would get you to negotiate his release. The second was that if I ever found myself in danger and he wasn't there for me, you and I were to go to the Double B and ask Del and your bad-boy buddies from fifteen years ago for their help.''

She tipped her chin firmly upward. ''Jess said the Double B was the only real home the four of you ever knew, whether you wanted to admit it or not.

You have to go home, Gabe. You have to take me and my baby daughter to the Double B, where we'll be safe.''

With the sleeveless black vest fitting him like a second skin and the white bandage slashing across the dark tan of his right shoulder, all at once the man facing her seemed unreachably remote. Silver glinted at his wrist as the swell of his biceps tensed.

He exhaled, and in the sound there was a hint of defeat.

''I'd like to think I might have been able to say no to you on this one, princess,'' he said brusquely. ''But I'm no match against you and Jess together. Get Emily ready for a helicopter ride.''

He strode past her to the doorway, his mouth a grim line. ''We leave for the Double B in fifteen minutes.''

THE DOUBLE B'S KITCHEN wasn't as spacious as he remembered, Gabe thought two hours later as he closed the door of the spare bedroom leading off from it, where he'd deposited his one bag of belongings. But maybe the seeming lack of space was an illusion, brought about by the fact that right now there wasn't a single empty chair at the scarred pine table that took center stage in the rustic room, beneath the antique hanging lamp and a few feet away from the equally old-fashioned cookstove. Tye's seat was close to that of his new wife, Susannah, while Connor had his arm around a slim Dineh woman he'd introduced as Tess, with whom he'd also recently tied the knot.

*Looks like you were well on your way to being the*

*last bachelor holdout of the original gang, Riggs, especially since even Hawkins is a married man now.* He frowned as the notion crossed his mind. *But once Jess had married Caro, wild horses wouldn't have dragged you to a Double B gathering like this one anyway. As it is, it took his death to accomplish that.*

Gabe steeled himself against the pain that slashed through him, and saw from the grim set of Tye's mouth and the bleak expression in Con's eyes that they were steeling themselves, too. Susannah and Tess, whom he'd gathered had both met Jess in the past two months, weren't attempting to emulate their spouses's foolish male stoicism, he noted. Like Caro earlier, they were allowing their tears to fall unheeded.

While she'd been bundling Emily into a carry-cot at the Lazy J and gathering the essentials she'd asked Mrs. Percy to pack for her daughter, he'd placed a call to the Double B to advise Hawkins of their arrival and the reason for it. He'd been surprised when Connor had answered the phone, and disconcerted to hear the genuine pleasure in his old friend's voice before he'd had a chance to break the news of Jess's death.

"Hell, Riggs, we figured you'd dropped off the edge of the world, man. You've missed three weddings, I'll have you know—mine, Tye's and, if you can believe it, Hawkins's—plus all the rest of the action that's been happening lately on the Double B. There's too much to tell you over the phone, but Tye and I and our better halves are now living here, as well as a couple of Del's old Beta Beta Force buddies from his Vietnam days—John MacLeish and Daniel

Bird, Tye's new father-in-law. Jess said he was going to find out where you'd disappeared to. Don't tell me the son of a gun finally did.''

''In a way,'' he'd answered with difficulty. ''I've got bad news, Con. Brace yourself.''

From the moment Caro had told him Jess had been kidnapped he'd known there was an outside chance of tragedy, as little as he'd wanted to acknowledge that possibility, Gabe thought somberly. But to the people sitting around this table now, Jess Crawford's murder had come without any warning at all. Even Daniel Bird and John MacLeish, Del's buddies and men who'd known Jess only slightly, seemed shaken and stunned, while Greta, Del's new wife, was openly weeping with the other women.

*Of course, Mr. Semper Fi himself didn't crack,* he thought with a flicker of anger. *When our helicopter landed in the field and he drove out to meet us in his Jeep, for all the emotion he showed he could have been back in 'Nam, greeting a new contingent of recruits, dammit. Even when Greta offered to show Caro to the room that had been prepared for her and Emily, Hawkins insisted on playing the hospitable ranch baron and getting her settled in himself.*

But what had he expected? Gabriel asked himself. The man was as tough as rawhide. Obviously not even the death of one of his former protegés touched—

''You're handling this well.''

Looking up, Gabe saw Tye filling a battered tin coffeepot at the sink beside him. As quiet as the observation had been, he thought he discerned a rebuke in it and responded sharply. "Hadn't you heard? I'm an old hand at losing hostages, Adams. Sure, this time it was a personal friend and I saw him killed right in front of my eyes, but what the hell. A few more like tonight and I might even manage the same iron-assed lack of reaction as Hawkins."

"I never thought I'd hear you call me your role model in anything, Riggs. In fact, I seem to remember you once told me I was the biggest son of a bitch you'd ever known."

Del's clipped tones came from the doorway that led from the kitchen to the hall. Beside him stood Caro, the dismay on her face evidence that she, too, had overheard his intemperate rejoinder to Tye.

Hawkins entered the room, his gray gaze flinty. "I'd say right now you've got me beat hands down in that category, though, boy. You want to take this outside and see?"

Jess had told him Del was walking again, Gabe recalled, courtesy of a pair of prosthetic legs that a few years ago had replaced the ones he'd lost when an explosion had robbed him of his own during the waning days of the long-ago war he and Bird and MacLeish had fought in. It was still unsettling to see him out of the wheelchair that had once been so much a part of him. *The old man looks good,* he told himself reluctantly. *And if we hadn't already butted heads I might even try to tell him I'm glad for him.*

But right now wasn't the moment. Right now Del Hawkins seemed to think Gabriel Riggs was still the sixteen-year-old punk whose butt the tough ex-marine, wheelchair or no wheelchair, had once whipped in an arranged fight out back behind the horse barn.

And right now Gabe needed to make it clear those days of *sir, yes sir!* were long over.

He grinned tightly at Hawkins, because he knew his grin had always riled the man. "Why not, Lieut? Don't they say a wake's like a wedding—it hasn't really gotten under way until a few punches get thrown? Behind the horse barn again?"

"You're on, boy," Del rumbled, striding toward the door that opened from the kitchen onto the ranch house's wraparound porch. "It'll be pure pleasure to show you that some things haven't changed around—"

"Stop right there, mister!" The barked command sounded as if it had come from a drill sergeant—a female drill sergeant, Gabe realized in astonishment as he saw Greta push her chair abruptly away from the table and take a swift step to block her husband's path. At the same moment, Caro advanced toward him, her expression coldly angry.

Both women spoke at once. Both voices could have peeled paint from a wall.

"What the *hell* do you think you're playing at, Delbert?"

Greta's incredulous query was all Gabe heard of her reaming-out of Del before Caro gained his attention by planting herself in front of him.

"Are you out of your *mind,* Gabe? Have you forgotten what brought us here?" Her gaze was chillier than Del's had been. "The only thing you got right was that this is in the nature of a wake—Jess's wake.

I won't allow you to turn it into a brawl!'' She pressed her lips together. "I want to see you march over to Del and shake his hand. And then the two of you can start acting like the adults you both are.''

"I couldn't have said it better myself,'' Greta snapped. "Go on, Del. Shake hands with Gabe and apologize.''

Gabe's glare met Del's equally recalcitrant one. He saw Del's jaw tighten stubbornly at the very moment his own clenched.

*I love it! The old man and Riggs, both of them getting reamed out by a pair of feisty females. Too sweet, man!* At first Gabe didn't know who the laughing voice in his head belonged to. Then it hit him, and suddenly the pain he'd been holding back all night was right there in his throat, making it impossible to speak. He saw the sheen he hadn't noticed before glazing Del's gray gaze, and slowly he extended his hand.

Del clasped it like a man grabbing a life buoy.

"You know who would have gotten one hell of a kick out of us behaving like damn fools and being put on report for it, Riggs?'' His voice was no longer frosty, it was rusty.

Gabe jerked his head in a nod. "I was just thinking that myself. Jess would have had a field day with this, wouldn't he?''

Del didn't answer. His grip on Gabe's hand tightened almost unbearably, and the unshed tears in his eyes became more than a sheen. "You're sure there's no way he might have—''

Gabe couldn't let him finish. "No way,'' he said

hoarsely. ''Point-blank shot to the temple. I—I saw his—'' He squeezed Del's hand as tightly as his was being gripped, and shook his head. ''No need for details, but it would have been instantaneous,'' he rasped. ''It was Jess's body those bastards drove away with, Del, not Jess. Caro's right, this is his wake.''

''I see.'' Del's lips moved once before he firmed them. He blinked, and it was as if the tears that had been standing in his eyes froze to a thin film of ice. He released Gabe's hand. ''That's that, then. One of our own is gone.''

It couldn't just be his Marine Corps training that made it possible for him to step so quickly back into his spit-and-polish persona, Gabe thought quizzically. Hell, Bird and MacLeish were leathernecks too, and they hadn't been able to hide their reactions anywhere near as well as their former lieutenant. Whatever ancestor of Del's had passed down the gene for flinty gray eyes and the dogged determination that had helped him survive the loss of both legs, had obviously also bequeathed to him a toughness that didn't allow for displays of emotion.

He forced the lump in his throat to disappear. When he answered Hawkins his voice was steady. ''Yeah, one of our own is gone. And like I told Tye when I phoned, there's a chance it won't end there. Caro and her baby have been threatened, which is why we're here.''

''Tye explained the situation.'' Hawkins's nod was curt. ''The Double B's already gone on full alert, Riggs. Joseph and Billy Tahe, who man the gate leading onto the property, have rounded up a few cousins from the Dinetah to beef up security on the ranch perimeter. Add to that the five able-bodied men right here in this room and a certain stiff-legged, iron-assed son of a bitch who can still fire a rifle pretty damn well, and I'd say we've got ourselves a tight setup.''

''Stiff-legged, iron-assed chauvinist,'' Greta interjected tartly. ''Susannah's a dead shot, and you know it, sweetie. Tess is no slouch with a handgun, either, and as a reclusive artist living on my own until recently, I got a crusty old ex-marine to show me how to handle a firearm, if you'll remember. But it's good to know us helpless females have you big strong males to protect us, especially since Susannah's got baby Danny to keep her busy and Tess has her hands full with that nine-year-old hell-raising nephew of hers.''

''Con's and my nine-year-old hell-raising adopted son, as soon as the paperwork goes through,'' the dark-haired woman who'd been introduced to Gabe as Tess smiled. Her smile faded. ''Jess dead, and over something as stupid as money. I still can't believe it.''

''I don't believe it.''

All eyes in the room, Gabe's included, turned to Tye at his unexpected contribution to the conversation. But Tye, Gabe noted with some of his old impatience at his friend, didn't continue immediately. As if it were a vital task, he lifted the coffeepot from the stove.

Gabe's impatience became irritation. ''You know, Adams,'' he drawled, ''it's a damn good thing you've given up your bodyguard-to-the-stars business out there in California and settled down here in New

Mexico with Susannah. Quit milking the scene and spill whatever it is you have to say. You've got your audience in the palm of your hand and you know it.''

Tye set the coffeepot down and faced him. ''Not milking the scene, bro,'' he said mildly enough that the hint of answering irritation in his voice was barely audible. ''I'm just wondering how crazy this is going to sound to the rest of you. I know it did to me when Jess told me, but now I'm not sure.''

''Jess was in touch with you?'' For the first time since she'd reamed him out, Caro spoke, her tone strained. Everything about her seemed strained, Gabe noticed, from the added pallor in her creamy complexion to the way her fingertips went unconsciously to the bare skin of his forearm, as if she suddenly needed to feel the warmth of another human being.

*And that surprises you, Riggs?* This time the voice in his head was his own, and it was roughly sardonic. *For a woman who's been protected from the seamier side of things for most of her life she came through the events of this evening like a trooper, but it has to have taken a toll on her. She saw the man she was going to marry killed. She nearly got killed herself. And now she's worried sick that her daughter might be the target of that bastard Leo. I'd say she's earned the right to a little strain.*

Which still didn't change the fact that having those slim fingers on him made it hard to concentrate, he admitted to himself reluctantly. Hell, just standing next to her made it difficult to concentrate, which was why he'd tried to keep his distance from her today, both physically and emotionally.

He was going to have to try harder, but not just yet. He covered her hand with his.

"When did you speak with him, Adams?"

"Three days ago. He was leaving for his Mexican trip, he said, so he didn't have much time to talk. But he asked me to set up a meeting with all the Double B's for when he got back."

Tye frowned. "Jess said he'd stumbled upon a link between everything that had happened recently at the ranch, and Del's past in Vietnam. He said it was all part of a bigger picture, and that if his guess was right, the Double B and everyone connected to it was in more danger than we could possibly imagine."

His frown turned into a scowl. "I think the kidnapping was a ruse. I think Jess was killed because of what he found out."

## Chapter Six

This time it wasn't Jess bound to the chair, Caro realized numbly, it was Gabe. And the gunman standing guard over him was Del—not Del as he was now, but Del as he would have been thirty years ago, when he'd been in Vietnam and, as she'd learned, part of a mysterious group called Beta Beta Force.

She knew it was a dream. She'd known it was a dream when it had come to her the night before, and the night before that, her first one at the Double B. But knowing didn't help. There was always some new and terrible twist she hadn't anticipated, and tonight was no exception.

The events played out with the same inexorable sense of doom they always did. The truck began to accelerate. Gabe's agonized gaze met hers one final time before lifting to the man standing over him. The young Del's face was a mask of pain and regret, but as if he had no choice in the matter, slowly he placed the barrel of the gun he was holding to Gabe's temple. Just as he began to pull the trigger, the night exploded in a firestorm of brilliant light and flames, and Caro, now holding Emily, tried to run from the inferno.

But she tripped instead over the briefcase full of bearer bonds and fell to the ground, screaming out her daughter's name as Emily flew from her arms...

Jerking bolt upright in bed, Caro flung the light cover back and sped across the pine-planked floor to Emily's crib a few feet away, the nearly full moon outside supplementing the dim illumination provided by the night-light she'd switched on earlier in the evening. She bent over the crib, her heart still thudding painfully in her chest and the residue of the nightmare clinging to her like tendrils of fog.

"What is it?"

The low query came from the darkness behind her. Whirling around, she choked back the scream that rose in her throat as a shadowy but instantly recognizable figure advanced.

"For goodness' sake, Gabe! I'm checking on Emily, that's all. And why were you lurking outside my bedroom door anyway?"

"I wasn't." His reply was still low-voiced. "I was inside, princess. You got a problem with that?"

"You were—"

In the hushed room her indrawn breath was sharp. Suddenly all too conscious of the thin nightdress she was wearing, Caro turned and padded swiftly to the bed. She slipped on the matching robe, knotting its tie-belt securely around her waist before confronting him again.

"Let me get this straight. You were in the room while I slept? You were *watching* me?"

"Watching over you." He sounded bored. "Don't

get all hot and bothered, princess. I certainly wasn't, if that's what you're thinking.''

He inclined his head at the screened window. ''Grappling hook over the sill, rudimentary climbing skills and a bottle of chloroform. That's all anyone would need to up the hostage count to include a mother and her child.''

''You're forgetting they'd have to transport me and Emily out a window and off the property,'' she snapped. ''I somehow don't think they'd find it all that easy to accomplish.''

''You're right,'' he agreed. ''Which means maybe they'd take the simpler alternative, honey. We know Leo doesn't draw the line at killing off his liabilities.''

His words effectively robbed her of any further desire to argue with him. With an effort Caro curbed the impulse to look over her shoulder at the window and the night outside.

''Why do you do that?'' she asked shakily. ''Why do you have to be so—so *blunt* when you're talking with me?''

''How else should I have phrased it? From what I know of Leo, he's a pretty blunt type. I wouldn't be doing you a favor to pretend otherwise.''

She shook her head. ''Even when I first met you. Even when the name Leo only belonged to a victim. When I left Larry's chalet with you and I asked why you'd thrown him down the stairs, you didn't just say he'd caused a man's death. You made a point of telling me that he'd been responsible for Roswell getting his throat cut, as if you needed to make it clear to me right from the start that your world was full of a violence I couldn't begin to comprehend. Why?''

Her vision had adjusted to the dim glow from the night-light enough by now that she could see his quick frown. He exhaled, and Caro was sure she heard a muttered oath beneath his sigh.

"I guess I do at that, princess." His admission took her aback. "Maybe I'm trying to make it clear to myself that your world and mine are miles apart. I know I was that first night anyway."

"You didn't have to, that first night. I threw up enough barriers to make sure you knew we had nothing in common, didn't I?" She bit her lip. "You called me a bitch. I was one."

Maybe it was the setting, she thought, holding his gaze. It was the middle of the night, the house was still, and the small pool of light from the fixture near the baseboard seemed to isolate them from the rest of the sleeping world. In the crib beside them Emily gave a peaceful little gurgle, followed by a tiny baby snore. Right now she and Gabe were just a man and a woman keeping watch over a child. Life didn't get much more basic than that, and somehow in such a situation the usual defenses and stilted subterfuges of conventional conversation fell away.

She could never be totally honest with him. But it was suddenly important to tell him one particular truth.

"The woman I was eighteen months ago..." she said, the corners of her lips attempting a smile. "If I met her today, I don't think I'd like her any more than you did, Gabe. I don't think I really liked her very much then.'' She looked away. ''I've always wanted to apologize to you for the horrible things I said the next morning. I tried to phone you a few weeks later, but you'd already dropped out of sight.''

She made an unnecessary adjustment to the light blanket covering Emily. ''It probably wouldn't have made any difference if I'd contacted you before you left, though, would it.''

''Probably not.'' Although his reply was characteristically blunt, the usual brusqueness was missing from his tone. ''I went to the desert hoping to find something. What happened between us just persuaded me to go looking for it a little sooner, that's all.''

This certainly was turning into a night for unexpected confidences, Caro thought. Why did that suddenly make her feel so off balance, so ill at ease?

*Because he's more dangerous like this.* The answer came promptly to her. *You can handle Gabriel Riggs when he's prickly, you can handle him when he's being tough, but you're absolutely defenseless against any hint of vulnerability from him. Fighting with the man is a whole lot safer than talking with him like this, so change the subject right now.*

Lightly she smoothed a wisp of hair from Emily's cheek. Equally lightly she traced the delicate line— so delicate it looked as if an artist had dipped the tip of a feather in ink and drawn it—of one tiny black eyebrow, and ignored the advice she'd just given herself.

''What were you looking for?''

''Myself.'' There was a touch of mockery in his reply. ''I guess I thought if the desert was good enough for madmen and saints, I didn't have anything to lose by giving it a shot.''

She looked up from her daughter with a slight frown. ''I don't understand.''

He shrugged. ''The job had been getting me down long before Roswell's death. I saw the worst of human nature on a daily basis, but I didn't have anything to weigh it against. That's against all precepts of the Middle Way, and I suppose I'm Navajo enough to think a life like that isn't a whole one.''

''The Middle Way?'' Her brow cleared. ''Of course. Balance and harmony in all things. It sounds like a good belief to me.''

''But you didn't have to go looking in the desert for something to hold on to, you found it when you became a mother.'' His gaze narrowed intently. ''I couldn't credit it at first, but over the past couple of days I've come to realize it's true. You have changed. This little sweetheart's the reason for that change, isn't she.''

''She's pure innocence, Gabe,'' Caro said simply. ''And just looking at her makes me want to be the best mother I can be—the best *person* I can be. Does that sound silly?''

''Not to me.'' He took a step toward the crib. ''In my line of work, sometimes it's a relief to see pure innocence once in a while. Can I?''

''Of— Of course.''

Her heart suddenly in her throat, she moved aside to make room for him. This was why she shouldn't have let her guard down with the man, she berated herself silently. This was exactly the situation she'd tried so hard to prevent, and now through her own incautiousness it was happening.

Avoiding letting Gabe spend any uninterrupted time with his daughter hadn't been too difficult. Since their arrival at the Double B he'd been preoccupied with bolstering the security measures at the ranch's perimeter, had been engaged in long and sometimes heated conversations with Del and Con, and had met with a couple of FBI agents—former colleagues of Con's from his days at the Bureau, apparently—to discuss Jess's kidnapping and murder. And although he'd made it clear that she and Emily were never to be alone and unprotected, it had been easy to arrange to take Emily outside for some fresh air only when Daniel Bird or John MacLeish had been assigned to guard them.

She hadn't hidden Emily away. She'd just been very careful not to give Gabe the opportunity to take the kind of long, searching look that Del had directed at her daughter yesterday—a look that had been re-placed by a quickly blank expression when the ex-marine had seen her watching him.

*The only thing that saved me then was that Del has no idea I knew Gabe before this week,* Caro thought faintly. *He saw something familiar in Emily, I'm sure of it. He just didn't realize that what he was seeing was something of Gabe.*

But Gabe would have to be blind not to recognize that straight little nose as a small facsimile of his own, the dark hair as coming from a Dineh daddy, the strong bones already giving definition to those rosy cheeks as being a delicate version of his own carved features.

And Gabe wasn't blind. So any moment now he would—

He reached into the crib, the bracelet on his wrist gleaming. Inscribed inside with his father's initials, it was all he had of the man he'd never known, apparently, just as a small enameled brooch-watch was all he had of his mother, Caro knew. Gently he extended his index finger toward one of Emily's tiny fists, and the next moment Caro saw it being clutched tightly by her still-sleeping daughter—almost as if the child knew there was a bond between them.

"She's beautiful." He looked up. "And she's not Kanin's daughter at all, is she."

Gently he disengaged his finger from Emily's grasp. He straightened to his full height, one side of his mouth lifting as he held Caro's frozen stare. "She's all you. Okay, I'll admit the dark hair had to have come from Larry, but she's a princess through and through, like her mama. God knows where she got that stern little nose from, though."

He looked down at Emily again. Caro's heart stopped for the second time as she saw the same uncompromising feature on his profile that he'd just noticed on his daughter.

"My father," she said swiftly, moving from the crib and hoping he would do the same. "She got the Moore nose. I only hope she didn't inherit the temperament to go along with it."

"What temperament would that be?"

In her relief at seeing him turn away from Emily,

Caro almost missed the wry undertone in his question. Belatedly she caught it, and managed a smile.

"The kind of temperament that leads to being dumped in a snowbank," she informed him. Her smile faded into uncertainty. "You said you'd seen a change, Gabe. I hope it's persuaded you that I can help you and the rest of the Double B contingent in trying to find out who was behind Jess's kidnapping and death, because I'm tired of sitting around twiddling my thumbs while everyone else is busy. Tyler's down in Mexico helping the *federales* search for Jess's body, Connor's in touch with the FBI, and Del's been holding hushed telephone conversations with his high-up military contacts. I know Greta's in Albuquerque on business, but Tess and Susannah have been running down some leads with the aid of Tess's reporter friends on the tabloid newspaper she used to write for. I'm the only one who isn't helping."

"Because you and Emily were the only ones specifically threatened by Leo." He'd started shaking his head even before she'd finished talking. "Maybe Jess's cryptic phone call before he left for Mexico convinced Tye there's more to this than a simple kidnapping gone wrong, but you remember what Jess was like. He was always getting all fired up over his latest enthusiasm. A month later he'd be excited over something new."

"Which was probably one of the reasons he became so successful in his field," she retorted. "He was willing to keep an open mind. But this wasn't like his short-lived mania for flying ultra-light planes, or his model railroad craze, Gabe. From what he told me after his two visits to the Double B in the past couple of months, the incidents that brought Susannah and Tyler together and then Connor and Tess, both left questions that were never satisfactorily explained. And Jess's curiosity was just as much a part of him as his enthusiasm, so he wouldn't simply have shrugged off those loose ends. What if he did learn something that put him in danger?''

''Something connected to Del's shadowy past in Vietnam?'' Gabe let out an impatient breath. ''For God's sake, that was over thirty years ago.''

He glanced around the softly lit room, and then seemed to come to a decision. ''Sit.''

With a nod at the rumpled bed, he pulled a nearby chair closer. As Caro reluctantly settled herself on the edge of the bed, he dropped into the chair and leaned forward, muscled forearms resting on his thighs, his hands hanging loosely between his knees.

''Has anyone filled you in on what Beta Beta Force was, exactly, and just how it was disbanded?''

She pressed her lips together. ''No,'' she replied with asperity. ''That's what I've been trying to tell you. Everyone's gone out of their way to make me welcome and comfortable here, but I still feel like an outsider.''

She saw the flicker of disconcertion that briefly crossed his face. ''You do, too. You and Del have kept things civil between you since the night we arrived, but the two of you still rub each other the wrong way. Is that why you don't want to explore Jess's theory?''

"I don't want to explore Jess's theory because I don't see the point," he replied shortly. "Look, Del and I aren't ever going to see eye to eye, but that doesn't mean I don't respect him for what he sacrificed in an unpopular and largely forgotten war. Beta Beta Force was a four-man covert operations group consisting of him, Daniel Bird, John MacLeish, and a man named Zeke Harmon. They were assigned to carry out the jobs that no one else would touch, and instead of being hailed as heroes when the war ended, any mention of their exploits was wiped from the official records."

"But all Del has to do is pick up the phone and he seems to be able to get through to any four-star general he wants," Caro protested. "That doesn't sound like he's been forgotten."

"Not by those who know the truth," Gabe conceded. "But to many, the name of Beta Beta Force was synonymous with one of the darkest chapters in American military history, and the four men who sported those tattoos you might have noticed on Del's or Daniel's or MacLeish's biceps—the tattoos depicting two bees fighting to the death—"

"Two bees?" A bell rang faintly in Caro's memory but echoed off into silence before she could place it. She shook her head at Gabe. "Sorry. Yes, I saw that tattoo on Daniel Bird's arm yesterday when he was sluicing off at the pump after working in the barn. I didn't realize Del and John MacLeish had identical ones. What's it supposed to represent, besides the obvious reference to the initials of their unit?"

"That any one of the four could count on the man

beside him to fight to the death for him. They were
as close as brothers in the beginning.'' He looked
down at his hands. ''But then rumors began to cir-
culate about a rogue killer who was murdering civilians, the enemy, and their own soldiers for sadistic
pleasure. The Double B's were assigned to track
down the killer, and when they did they found he was
one of their own—Zeke Harmon. They turned Harmon in to the authorities.''

She'd earlier accused him of being too blunt. But
she knew that in retelling this tragedy, Gabe had deliberately left out the gruesome details, and she found
herself suddenly grateful that he had. She swallowed.

''Learning that one of their number was a monster
must have torn the others apart, especially if they
were a band of brothers at the start, like you say.'' A
thought occurred to her, and her eyes widened. ''But
that could be what Jess discovered, Gabe. Maybe this
Harmon's been released after all these years and he's
looking for revenge on his old comrades.''

''So he targets a software billionaire who has a
peripheral connection to Del, and then threatens a
woman and child Hawkins doesn't know.'' His tone
was dry. ''Even if there was any logic to that, it
wouldn't wash. Harmon was killed, Caro. Del killed
him.''

''But—''

''But he was turned in to the authorities? Yeah, and
then the bastard escaped into the jungle he knew so
well.'' Gabe grimaced. ''By then Beta Beta Force had
been disbanded and Daniel Bird had actually been

shipped home, so Del and MacLeish were given the assignment to find Harmon and bring him back.''

He lifted broad shoulders in a shrug. ''They split up, Del found Harmon first, and when Harmon drew his gun, Del was forced to shoot to kill. A second later as he approached Zeke's body, he stepped on a booby trap the bastard had rigged. Obviously Harmon had planned to go out taking one of his old buddies with him. Only the fact that MacLeish found Del and carried him back to base camp twenty-five miles on his back saved Del's life, although not his legs.''

It had been over thirty years ago, as he'd said, Caro thought. But neither the passage of time nor Gabe's toneless recitation of the facts could lessen the horrific impact of the story she'd just heard. She saw one last possibility.

''Could there be a chance Harmon didn't die from Del's bullet? Was his body ever recovered?''

''We're talking jungle conditions. What was left of it was, along with his dog tags, a few days later.'' Gabe's smile was brief. ''You're like Jess, princess. You don't give up easy, do you.''

''Never say die,'' she agreed, trying to match his smile and failing as the aching sadness that had caught her unawares several times over the past forty-eight hours engulfed her again. She blinked back the moisture in her eyes. ''I'm with Connor's wife, Tess. I don't want to believe a good man like Jess was killed over something so senseless as money. Not that any reason would be acceptable for murder, but knowing there was one might stop me from seeing him every night in my dreams, bound to a chair in that fruit delivery van with a gun—''

''Fruit delivery van?'' Gabe's voice was sharp. ''How do you know that's what it was?''

''What do you mean, how did I know? You were there, too. You saw the—'' Caro paused. ''Or maybe you didn't,'' she said slowly. ''You were near the front of the truck when it stopped, and the glare of the headlights would have been in your eyes. When you moved around to the side, the opened panel door had slid across. But from where I was first standing by the SUV, I could—''

Her breath caught in her throat. The bell that had rung so faintly in her mind a few minutes earlier sounded again, and this time it was loud and clear.

''My knowledge of Spanish isn't anywhere near as good as yours,'' she said huskily. ''But I can recognize simple words. Gabe, the logo on the side of that truck was Dos Abejas Fruit Company. Doesn't that mean—''

His voice cut across hers before she could finish. ''The Two Bees, dammit,'' he said harshly. ''As in the Double B—and as in Beta Beta Force.''

## Chapter Seven

"You certainly set the cat among the pigeons last night, darlin'." Crossing the yard from the direction of the horse barn and catching sight of Caro sitting on the porch, Emily in her stroller beside her, a crease appeared in the tan of Del's cheek as he delivered his dry comment.

As he reached them he nodded at the man standing behind her. "That salve you put on the colt's leg seems to be doing the trick, Mac, but I think we'll keep him quiet for one more day. I saw an impatient-looking nine-year-old sitting in your truck waiting for you, said you'd promised to drive him into Last Chance to get some new boots. You'd better hustle along and let me take over here."

"Joey, Tess and Con's young hell-raiser." John MacLeish grinned at Caro. "I made the mistake of telling him a real cowboy needed real cowboy boots, and he's got his heart set on a pair he saw in the window of Hoyt's General in town."

It didn't necessarily take a village to raise a child, Caro thought with a smile as Del and John exchanged a few words beside her—it just took a ranch. The

Double B was proof of that, though right now the bunkhouse that during the school year held the current crop of wayward teens sent here to turn their lives around was only occupied by MacLeish and Daniel Bird. The men were using it for sleeping quarters while the houses that had been planned for them were being built on the opposite side of the sprawling ranch property from the two homes recently constructed for Tyler's and Connor's families.

"Gabriel's own damn fault, though," Del grunted, breaking open the rifle handed to him by MacLeish as the other man left the porch. He squinted briefly inside the weapon and locked the barrel into place again. "It might have occurred to him to ask you if you'd seen anything he hadn't at the scene that night. Did he tell you our old sad story, honey?"

His question was offhand, but Caro sensed her reply was important to him. "Gabe told me. It *is* a sad story, Del."

"Sadder still for Harmon's victims and the families they left behind," he said with a thread of remembered anger in his voice. "It was terrible enough back then to get a telegram informing you that your son or husband or fiancé had fallen in action, but to learn he'd been killed by a rogue murderer—" He shook his head. "No wonder some of the boys tarred all Beta Beta Force with the same brush. We should have figured out sooner that Zeke had crossed over to the darkness."

The very intensity of his muttered words told Caro this was a recrimination he'd berated himself with before. She hastened to turn his thoughts. "I didn't have the chance to speak with Gabe before he left with Connor this morning for the FBI field office in Albuquerque. How convinced is he that my information could mean Jess's kidnapping and murder was the start of a vendetta against anyone connected with you?''

''Not very, although he agreed with Con that going through the most-wanted files with an eye to age and military service was a step he couldn't skip.'' Del scowled. ''But like he said, if a disgruntled veteran's been holding a grudge against our unit for the death of a friend in 'Nam at the hands of Harmon, why has he waited so long to take revenge on us? Sure, Daniel's been in prison for the past fifteen years after being convicted of killing the scumbag who raped and murdered his wife, and Mac's been living in the shadows until recently, but anyone looking to hunt me down would have had an easy time of it. I was confined to a bed in a V.A. hospital for the first six months after being shipped home, and for another year after that, I was in a physical rehab program.''

She'd meant to divert him with her question, but Caro found her own attention momentarily straying. ''I can't imagine how hard that must have been for you,'' she said softly, ''and yet you went on to carve out a new life—and in the process turned the lives of countless teens in a more positive direction. Jess always said he thought of you as the only father he'd ever known.''

''Don't be too fast to pin a halo on me, honey.'' Salt-and-pepper eyebrows lifted. ''I was one surly ex-marine for the longest time, I can tell you. If it hadn't been for a rehab nurse who not only wouldn't let me quit but restored my sense of self-worth by giving me the greatest gift a woman could give a—"

He stopped abruptly, seemingly lost in his own thoughts. There was a story there, Caro thought curiously, and although it was a story that Del apparently wasn't prepared to share, it wasn't too hard to guess at the gist of it. She put her musings aside as he shot her a wry smile.

"Let's just say there was a time when I didn't think I was going to get my life back on track. And even after I did, Jess's high opinion of me never jibed with Gabriel's, as I'm sure you've noticed."

"I've noticed the two of you are always at odds with each other, probably because neither of you ever backs down from a position," she said tartly. "I've heard Greta call you her tough old mustang, and Gabe's as much a maverick as that bad-tempered Appaloosa, Chorizo, who's such a legend here at the Double B. Two stallions in one herd can't help but lead to the kind of testosterone-fueled displays you men indulged in the night we arrived."

She fixed him with a stern glare. A heartbeat later she clapped her hands to her mouth, appalled. "Del, I'm sorry. I had no right to speak to you the way I just did. I—I don't know what I thought I was doing."

He grinned at her. "You thought you were telling off our boy Gabriel, honey." His grin faded. "Hell, I know I ride him harder than I ever rode any of the others who came here," he growled. "When he was a teen I told myself it was because I saw so much potential in him, and I was afraid he was going to throw it all away."

"But he's a man now," she reminded him. "And he lived up to his potential, Del."

He shook his head. "Not fully. Not yet. Maybe that's why I'm still riding herd on him—because I'm still afraid he's going to let the life he could have slip through his fingers."

His gaze held hers. "A man needs roots. Maybe Gabe could have put down some if he'd gotten in touch with his Dineh heritage, but he's always been too much of a loner to do that. A wife and a child would complete him."

*He knows,* Caro thought, unable to turn from the gray eyes watching her. It didn't matter that Del Hawkins didn't have the full details of her involvement with Gabe; he knew just by looking at the baby girl napping in the stroller between them who Emily's father was. The question was, would he feel it was his duty to tell Gabe?

"His mother was killed by a hit-and-run driver when he wasn't much older than your little girl is now, and he was bounced around in the foster system after that," Del went on, still watching her. "He grew up fast and he grew up tough. Maybe someone of your social background might see Gabriel Riggs as no more than a man to call on when you need protection or muscle, but not one you'd consider a future with. A woman who thought that would be wrong."

With an effort she wrenched her gaze from his. Bending to the stroller, she adjusted its shade against the afternoon sun and spoke without looking at him.

"If it was his background that bothered her, then of course that woman would be wrong. But what if the reason she didn't see a future with Gabe was that he'd shown her in every way he knew how, that he didn't want those roots you say he needs? Would she still be wrong? Would you still be so quick to pass judgment on her, Del?"

She gave up all pretense. "Oh, Gabe wouldn't shirk his responsibilities," she said unhappily. "If he knew Emily was his daughter, he'd feel duty-bound to acknowledge her. He's too decent a man not to, and besides, he obviously feels a connection to her, even if he doesn't know why."

"So what's the problem?"

She looked up sharply. "The problem is that roots can't be grafted. You said it yourself—if Gabe truly wanted to put down roots, he would have gotten in touch with his Dineh heritage before now. He would have made his peace with you and the Double B. My little girl deserves to be more than a responsibility to the man she calls Daddy. She should be his sun and his moon and his stars, like she is mine. Because if she isn't, one day she's going to realize it and the realization's going to tear her apart. I won't let that happen to her, Del. I'd rather bring her up without a father."

She stared stonily at him. "Are you going to tell him?"

Slowly he shook his head. "No, I won't tell him if you don't want me to. But it's just a matter of time before he sees it for himself."

"Not if Emily and I are out of his life before he

can,'' she replied dully. ''And that's the plan. As soon as I know my daughter's safe again, I intend to walk away from Gabriel Riggs for the second time in my life—this time for good.''

''And if he comes after you—''

He didn't finish the rest of his question. His lean body suddenly tense, slowly he rose from his chair and narrowed his eyes in the direction of the dirt road leading to the yard.

''What—''

He cut across her query, his voice low and flat. ''Take Emily out of her stroller, honey, and get into the house.'' She blinked at him, and harshly he added, *''Now!''*

The urgency in his tone galvanized Caro into action. Scooping Emily up, she hastened to the screen door that opened from the porch to the kitchen. Stepping inside, she pulled it securely shut before looking out at Del.

He was already sighting down the barrel of the rifle. She followed his gaze, and saw a weaving gray shape approaching from across the yard.

For the first time in her life Caro realized that the tiny hairs on the back of her neck actually could rise. ''What's the matter with that dog? Why is it stumbling?''

''It's rabid.'' Del didn't take his attention from the advancing animal. He swore under his breath. ''That's Chuck Weatherby's bluetick hound, Jake. Chuck told me a couple of days ago that Jake had gone missing, and he was worried a wolf had got him. Cover your baby's ears, honey.''

Caro complied, hugging a now-fretting Emily to her breast and fumbling the light blanket in which she was swaddled up around her head. Her precautions came just in time. A moment later the explosive *crack* of a rifleshot rang out, so shockingly loud that pain lanced Caro's eardrums.

Emily began to cry. Caro's gaze flew to the animal, now lying motionless in the yard.

"Stay here while I take care of the body," Del muttered. "Where are my gloves?"

Setting the rifle down, he slapped the back pocket of his jeans. Caro, attempting to soothe Emily, shook her head.

"You didn't have them when you came from the barn." She wasn't surprised to hear the quaver in her voice.

"Must have left them there." His glance lit on an oil-stained scrap of leather that MacLeish had earlier used to wipe the rifle's stock. Grabbing it up along with his cane, he made his way down the porch steps.

The episode, although quickly over, had been upsetting, Caro admitted to herself. And it could have turned out much more tragically if Tess's nine-year-old Joey had been playing nearby with his puppy and inseparable companion, Chorrie. Feeling suddenly limp with reaction, she dropped a fiercely thankful kiss on the top of Emily's silky hair.

*"Hell!"*

Del's unexpected oath jerked her attention back to him, and she looked up just in time to see him take a quick step backward. The dog's foaming jaws snapped on empty air, its neck stretched rigidly back, and then its head fell to the dirt again. It shuddered once, and was still.

"Of all the greenhorn stunts to pull." This time it was Del's voice that wasn't entirely steady. He grimaced at the bleeding gash on his wrist. "He's dead now, but he had one last bite in him, dammit. I should have known better than to handle him without gloves."

"We've got to get you to a hospital." Her concern for him overriding her nervousness, Caro pushed open the screen door and descended the porch steps. "Emily's infant seat is in Greta's four-by-four. I'll drive."

"I'll be okay until Mac or Daniel or one of the women return." Under Del's tan, his face was gray. "I'd better find something to bind this—"

"Lieutenant Hawkins, you're seeing a medic and that's final," she ordered. "Not only do you need a rabies shot, but that bite's too ragged to heal properly unless it's stitched. Isn't there a doctor in Last Chance?"

"Gabe didn't want you going into town. Too open. Too public," he said between gritted teeth. "But you're right, I should get this seen to. The closest medical facility is Joanna Tahe's clinic. I'll give you directions on the way."

His grin was wan. "I guess Emily's going to have her first brush with the other half of her heritage, honey. Joanna's Dineh, and her clinic's on the Dinetah—the Navajo Nation, where Gabe's ancestors on his mother's side came from."

"DEL'S STUBBORN, but I'm used to dealing with stubborn patients." Joanna Tahe entered the clinic's reception area where Caro, a sleepy Emily in her arms, was waiting. "Admittedly most of them don't use cuss words while I'm giving them a needle, but that's probably because their vocabularies are still too limited."

Caro mustered a smile. "Even if Del hadn't told me this was a clinic for new mothers and their babies, I would have guessed from the decor." She nodded at the wallpaper frieze of bunnies that ran along the top of the wall. "How's he doing, Joanna?"

The trim, dark-haired woman had insisted Caro call her by her first name within moments of their meeting, but her lack of formality hadn't overshadowed her crisp professionalism as she'd taken charge of Del. Over his protests, she'd whisked him into her examination room—normally occupied by her usual kind of patient, she'd explained briefly, but since this was the hour she usually caught up on her paperwork, luckily it and the waiting room were empty.

"The bite was deeper than it looked, but I did a tidy embroidery job on it, if I do say so myself." Joanna smiled. "Don't worry, he'll be fine. Antirabies treatment has come a long way from the old days, but I want him to rest before making the drive home, so I gave him a mild sedative that will help him drift off for a while. That works out well for what I'm about to suggest, actually."

She held out her arms for Emily. "May I?"

Without hesitation Caro deposited the little girl into the other woman's arms. Joanna Tahe was a naturally mothering type, Caro thought as the nurse bent her head to Emily's with a soft murmur. It explained her choice of profession and the success she'd made of it.

"*Nali* has been asking me to arrange for you to see her." Joanna lifted her gaze from the baby in her arms and met Caro's questioning glance. "Sorry. *Nali* is the Dineh word for grandmother, and although Alice Tahe's my great-grandmother, I grew up calling her that. She's a very old lady—and stubborn," she added dryly.

"Your cousin Joseph works as security on the Double B, right?" As the nurse nodded, Caro went on. "I've talked with him once or twice when he's come up to the house. He's told me about her. She sounds like a wonderful person."

"Wonderful but with a will of iron. And she holds firmly to the old beliefs," Joanna added. "News travels fast on the Dinetah. When she learns you were here, she's going to ask why I didn't insist you stop by to take tea with her. Apparently she has something important she wants to tell you."

Her lips turned down ruefully. "Please don't feel you have to, Caro. I just wanted to be able to tell her with a clear conscience that I'd passed on her message to you." She shook her head. "I have an idea of what it is she thinks you need to hear from her. Over the past few months she's been buttonholing everyone she can who has a connection to the Double B and trying to convince them there's a—"

She paused. Caro frowned in polite inquiry.

"That there's a what?" she asked.

Joanna didn't answer her directly. "You couldn't

be any more *Belacana* if you tried, could you.'' Her
tone was teasing, but not unkindly so. ''Non-Navajo,
I mean. Long blond hair, blue eyes. If it weren't for
this little sweetie pie in my arms, I'd assume you'd
never had any connection with our culture and people,
and I wouldn't bother telling you about an old Dineh
lady and her beliefs. But Emily makes me think you
might understand.''

Her voice softened. ''I told you news travels fast
here, and I knew Jess well enough to mourn his loss
when I heard of his death. Your secrets will remain
on the Dinetah—both the fact that you're hiding out
on the Double B while the danger to you is dealt with,
and what I as a Dineh woman see in your baby, Caro.
The father doesn't know?''

''The father can't know,'' Caro said through frozen
lips. ''Del guessed. Now you have. Is it so obvious?''

''Dineh babies are my life's work, so I'm a hard
one to fool on the subject. And when you get to know
Del better, you'll learn that those hawk eyes of his
see a lot farther than most people's.'' Joanna sighed.
''But to get back to *Nali*. She's convinced there's an
evil spirit or ghost—she calls it Skinwalker—threatening the Double B. She blames the recent incidents
that have happened on this evil, though both times
it's turned out the trouble has been from human
sources.''

''The man who went there to kill Susannah Bird,
and the people who were after Tess and young Joey.''
Caro nodded, puzzled. ''Jess helped out in both instances, and he told me a little about them at the time.

But even if your great-grandmother thinks this Skin-walker was involved, why does she want to talk to me?''

''Probably because you're the only one she hasn't told her story to yet.'' Joanna's lips lifted ruefully. ''Her hogan—that's a traditional-style Dineh home—isn't far, and you can leave Emily here with me…but again, if you'd rather not go—''

''I don't mind.'' Caro returned her smile. ''On our way to your clinic Del told me I'm probably safer on the Dinetah than at the ranch, since strangers stick out like a sore thumb here. And I owe you, Joanna,'' she added softly, ''not just for looking after Del so well, but for keeping my secret about Emily to yourself. How do I get to Alice Tahe's hogan?''

ONE STRAIGHT ROAD. Then two well-marked turns. How hard should that have been? Caro asked herself in frustration half an hour later. *Face it, you're lost,* she thought. *And to top everything off, it looks like it's about to rain.*

No sooner had the thought gone through her mind than the first fat drop splatted against the windshield of the pickup, followed by a second and a third. Almost instantly the downpour came in earnest, rattling on the roof of the truck so loudly that she felt as if she were in a drum.

''There's got to be somewhere I can turn around here,'' she muttered, peering with difficulty through the streaming windshield and awkwardly shifting the truck into a lower gear. What would really help, she thought, would be another vehicle showing up—preferably one with a driver obliging enough to guide her back to the main road where—

As if some indulgent genie had heard her request, a pair of headlights appeared in her rearview mirror. With a sigh of relief she slowed the truck even more and started to pull to the side of the road, with the intention of flagging down her benefactor as he drew alongside.

But that wasn't going to happen, she realized as she saw the speed at which he was approaching. In fact, if she hadn't switched on her own lights to cut through the sudden grayness, her main concern right now would have been to make sure he was aware of her presence in time to avoid running into her.

The lights loomed larger. She wasn't aware she had been holding her breath until at the last moment the vehicle swung out to pass her and she allowed herself to exhale again.

"Of all the—" Shaky anger filled her as the pickup pulled level with her. Her hands wrapped around the steering wheel, she darted a furious glance at the driver.

His features were obscured by a ball cap pulled low on his forehead, but the cap itself was vaguely familiar. Caro switched her attention back to the road with a frown. A gothic-style letter *D*. Didn't that stand for—

The steering wheel was jerked out of her grip as the truck swerved violently into her.

## Chapter Eight

Caro frowned through half-closed eyes. The cardboard pine tree that hung from the four-by-four's rearview mirror was dangling the wrong way. There was a tight pressure at the top of her left shoulder and another constriction around her hips. What was going on?

Her head hurt, and trying to think made it hurt more. Whatever had happened, she could figure it out later, she told herself. Right now she felt like drifting off to sleep again, if only someone would turn down the annoying crackling noise that was coming from outside.

She closed her eyes. Darkness, warm and comforting, rushed back to claim her. The crackling became louder.

Panic slammed into her, jolting her out of drowsiness and into cold awareness. She'd been in an accident. A pickup truck had run her off the road. She remembered fighting with the steering wheel, remembered feeling the tires lose traction and seeing the rain-dark horizon rotating crazily in front of the windshield. Then all vision had been cut off by the air bag deploying as the four-by-four had come to a violent and upside-down halt in the ditch by the side of the road.

How long had she been hanging here, supported by her shoulder and lap belts like some topsy-turvy sky diver with the now-deflated air bag as her parachute? And what *was* that crackling noise anyway?

The last of the fogginess clouding her brain cleared. A second later she burst into terrified action, her right hand scrabbling furiously at the latch of her seat belt and the fingers of her left straining for the door handle beside her.

The engine was on fire. She had to get out *now,* Caro thought in cold fear. But to get out she had to release the seat belt, and it wasn't unlatching. What was she doing wrong?

Nothing, she realized a thudding heartbeat later. The latch was jammed. She was trapped inside a vehicle that could explode into a fiery mass of flames at any moment.

"Dear God, *no.*" As the stricken moan came from her throat, hysteria lent a desperate edge to her efforts to free herself. Through the windshield the fugitive flames outlining the edges of the hood were an ominous indication of the conflagration she couldn't see, but that would be shooting up through the undercarriage of the inverted four-by-four.

*You're going to die here. You're never going to touch Emily again, never going to see her grow up. You'll never be able to tell Gabe how you felt the morning you woke up in his arms. He'll never know that you fell in love with him—that you died loving him.*

Was that true? Just for a moment her fingers froze into immobility. It was *true,* Caro thought slowly. It had been true the morning she'd walked out of his life, true throughout those eighteen long months without him, true when she'd found him again and asked for his protection for her and the child they'd created together. And he would never know, just as he would never know from her that Emily was his daughter.

*Maybe knowing how I felt wouldn't have made any difference to him. What I told Del today was right— if Gabe wanted roots he would have put some down before now. But at least my final moments on this earth wouldn't be filled with the knowledge that I'd been a coward, too afraid of my emotions to acknowledge them.*

Her hand fell from the seat-belt latch. She squeezed her eyes shut against the stinging smoke now filling the vehicle's interior, took a shallow breath and felt her lungs revolt against the acrid substitute for oxygen she'd drawn in.

This was the end, she thought hazily. She'd been run off the road by a maniac who probably hadn't bothered to look back at the accident he'd caused. She hadn't even seen his face.

Her thoughts drifted off into nothingness. Behind her closed eyelids she visualized a dim image of a man's hand, his wrist banded with gleaming silver, one tanned finger encircled by a baby's grasp...

"Wake up, pretty mama. I'd better get you out of

here before that long blond hair burns right off your head.''

The unfamiliar voice barely penetrated her consciousness, but the heavy, open-handed slap that accompanied them did. A second hard slap across her face shocked her into taking a breath—a breath of blessedly fresh air, Caro realized as her lungs greedily pulled in another one, and then a third.

''I had to kick out the window, so watch out for glass. Hold still while I cut you free.''

Though the smoke had cleared, it was impossible to see the face of her rescuer, but as he spoke, Caro heard a sound like a knife blade being opened. That was exactly what it was, she realized as something flashed through the gloom and the belt that had been digging into the top of her shoulder suddenly released. The blade flashed again and the bottom half of her body fell free. Immediately she began pushing against the dashboard with her feet in a frenzied attempt to wriggle out of the window, but even as she felt her rescuer pull her toward him, her head jerked painfully backward.

''My *hair*,'' she croaked. ''A piece of my hair's caught!''

''Calm down, sweetness.''

He'd obviously gulped in his share of smoke, too, because his voice was even hoarser than hers. It sounded clogged, as if there were stones grating together in his throat. But what he sounded like didn't matter. All that was important was that he was drawing her swiftly through the shattered window, having somehow disentangled the strand of hair that had held her back.

He was enormously strong, she realized. Before she could find her footing she felt herself being slung over a broad shoulder, a muscular arm clamping across the back of her knees to secure her. Even as her gaze took in the flames shooting through the storm-dark gloom from the inverted four-by-four, the man holding her began sprinting at top speed away from the blazing vehicle.

And not a moment too soon.

The explosion came with no warning, a towering pillar of orange boiling into the air. From her ignominous vantage point Caro saw the pillar waver, steady, and then collapse upon itself like some predator crouching to spring. Then it *did* spring.

A wall of heat and noise rushed at them. With a final effort her unknown rescuer made the other side of the road ahead of the racing curtain of fire and, covering her body with his own, turned his last leap into a tumbling roll. As his dive took them into the opposite ditch, she felt the searing heat pass over them and then recede.

''Guess tonight wasn't your time to die, pretty lady.'' The oddly unpleasant voice was only inches away from her ear, but in the shadows he was no more than a dark shape. ''Count yourself lucky that I came along.''

He'd saved her life, Caro told herself. If not for his actions, the four-by-four would have been her funeral pyre. So why was the uppermost desire in her mind an almost hysterical need to put as much distance as possible between her and that terrible, grating whisper?

"I—I was lucky," she agreed unevenly. "I can't thank—"

Suddenly he was no longer holding her, but instead had pulled away, his head tipped to one side. A moment later she sensed rather than saw him look down at her, and before she realized what he was doing he bent swiftly to her again.

"Company's coming." His mouth was so close to her ear that she could feel his lips moving as he spoke. "Time for me to go. Thanks for the memento, pretty one."

"Memento?"

But already he'd risen fluidly to his feet. Looking toward the road, Caro saw bright headlights speeding closer before she turned her attention back to her rescuer.

"What do you mean—"

He was gone as completely as if he had never been there, she saw with a shock. But why had he left so abruptly, and where was his own vehicle?

She didn't care, she thought with sudden vehemence. She owed him her life, but she never wanted to see him again—not that she actually had, now that she thought about it.

"There was something *wrong* about him," Caro said out loud. "It wasn't only the way he spoke to me, although that was part of it. He just seemed…"

*Evil.* That was the word she wanted to say, she realized as she got to her feet and took a stumbling step toward the road. The pickup came to a rocking halt behind the four-by-four, and Gabe leapt out.

"Gabe!"

At the sound of her voice he turned, his features drawn. He ran to her, catching her as her knees buckled.

"Dammit, Caro, when I saw the fire—"

He didn't finish his muttered sentence, instead wrapping her in an embrace so tight it was almost bone-crushing. She could fall apart now, she told herself. She was in Gabe's arms, her ordeal was over, and she could fall completely to pieces if that was what she wanted. Or she could just stand here and feel the tension trembling along his every muscle and listen to the rapid beat of his heart....

She chose the latter, pressing her cheek to the solid wall of his chest and barely noticing the rain trickling down the bare nape of her—

She stiffened in shock. The next moment she was pushing herself from Gabe, her movements clumsy with urgency. Her hands flew to her head, and tremblingly she smoothed her hair back past her temples, behind her ears, to her neck.

And felt the hacked-off ends—not just the single strand that had been caught as she'd been exiting the four-by-four, but all of it.

"He cut off my hair!" Horror rose in Caro, making it difficult to force the rest of her words out. "He took it with him, Gabe—as a *memento!*"

"Del's Greta was a supermodel before she quit ten years ago in her early thirties and began concentrating on painting.'' Susannah, Tye's wife, stepped back from a seated Caro, frowned and used the tips of the scissors to make one last careful snip. ''Since you didn't want to wait for her to do this when she returns home tomorrow from her Albuquerque gallery showing, I figured having her talk me through it on the phone was the next best thing. What do you think, Tess?''

Connor's wife looked thoughtful. ''I think it might just suit you better this way, Caro. Have a look.''

The Double B women were doing their best to raise her spirits, Caro thought, listlessly taking the hand mirror that Tess was holding out to her and allowing Susannah to swivel her chair around to face the big mirror over the dresser. Upon her return to the ranch an hour ago, after hearing a truncated version of her ordeal from a grim-faced Gabe, Susannah had whipped off the apron she'd been wearing to prepare supper and she and Tess had hustled Caro into the bedroom. While Susannah had been trying to contact Greta, who hadn't been at the art gallery but whom Susannah had finally tracked down at her hotel, Tess had taken care of Emily's evening bottle.

Neither woman had asked for details about what had happened, and for that she was grateful. She was going to have to talk about it eventually, but right now it was all she could do to keep herself under some semblance of control—and what had left her most shaken wasn't the accident, but the inexplicable action her rescuer had taken.

*Susannah and Tess understand that,* Caro thought.

*Any woman would. What that man did to me was a violation.*

Her reaction had nothing to do with vanity, and everything to do with feeling powerless. It had been a type of rape. With little interest she looked in the dresser mirror and saw a stranger staring back at her.

Caro Moore had had patrician good looks, she thought slowly. Pale hair had swept straight from an alabaster brow to fall in a smooth satin flow halfway down her back. Sometimes it had been twisted into a low chignon or held in place with a plain clasp, but it had always given an icily fragile, touch-me-not impression.

The stranger in the mirror didn't look fragile or princesslike at all. Edgy bangs skimmed arched eyebrows. Chunky layers swung freely inches above her shoulders. She looked as if she would be equally at ease whether in buttery black leather and slightly tight jeans or a designer suit and pearls.

The stranger in the mirror didn't look powerless. She looked sexy and tough and like a force to be reckoned with. She looked strong, Caro decided. Better than that, she *felt* strong. Strong and—

"And damn *mad*," she said, her voice low and determined. "Mad enough to stop letting everyone shunt her off to the sidelines and start taking an active part in this investigation. Mad enough to want to kick some Leo butt, darn it!"

In the mirror she saw Susannah and Tess exchange looks.

"Is this what they call girl power?" Susannah asked.

Tess shook her head. "It's what they call becoming a Double B bad babe, Suze. You and I went through it. Now it looks as though Caro here's joined us— and you know what?"

In the mirror her gaze met Caro's, and a slow grin spread over her features. "I get the feeling that Emily's mama just might prove to be the toughest of all us Double B females."

IT HAD BEEN HARD ENOUGH keeping his equilibrium around her when she'd been a snow princess, Gabe thought, casting a glance across the kitchen table at Caro as she lifted her coffee cup and nodded at something Connor was saying. But with that almost-platinum hair falling into her eyes and curving toward her lips, whatever equilibrium he'd once had where Caro Moore was concerned was all shot to hell.

It wasn't just the hair. He'd never seen her in anything more casual than tailored slacks and a bandbox-crisp blouse, but now she was wearing jeans, and with a sleeveless T-shirt, no less. The T-shirt showed off her arms and her arms showed off the honey glow her skin had taken on over the past few days at the ranch. But as unsettling as those details were, they were surface differences.

The real change was in her attitude. Elbows planted on the table, she took a bite of one of the homemade peanut-butter cookies Susannah had set out with the after-supper coffee. She frowned, pointed the cookie at Connor and interrupted him in the middle of a sentence, her words muffled.

"You're wrong, Con. I didn't get a good look at

the jerk who ran me off the road, but he wasn't the same person as the man who pulled me out of the car.'' She swallowed and her words became clearer. ''Before I lost control of the wheel, something struck me as familiar about the other driver. It's making me crazy that I can't remember what it was, darn it.''

''Don't beat yourself up about it, darlin','' Del said dryly. ''The vehicle you were in was rammed, you were trapped in a burning wreck, and your rescuer turned out to be a sicko. No one would blame you if you'd blanked out everything.''

''Me blanking out won't help us catch a killer, and that's what I intend to do from now on—help,'' Caro said. ''Leo had Jess killed. He's threatened my child's life. I won't stand idly by to let others handle this problem for me anymore.''

''Yeah, you will.'' Since no one else seemed to want to set her straight, Gabe thought, it looked as though the job had fallen to him by default. ''Like I told you before, you're out of this precisely because you *are* a target. Your recklessness today could have cost you your life, dammit—and if you're too stubborn to see that, Del should have.''

''Riggs is right. I put you in danger by getting you to drive me to Joanna's,'' Hawkins said gruffly. ''It was a bone-headed play on my part.''

It wasn't the response Gabe had expected from the ex-marine, but before he could reply, Caro cut in, her tone sharp.

''I insisted you get medical attention, Del, and I'd make the same decision again. What happened to me on the Dinetah was no one's fault but my own, and

I'll thank both you and Gabe to let me take responsibility for my actions like the adult I am. I shouldn't have driven off to find Alice Tahe's hogan by myself, granted. That doesn't mean I can't—"

"Alice Tahe?" Tess sounded startled. "I didn't realize you were on your way to see her when the accident happened."

This conversation was getting away from the point he needed to make, Gabe told himself. He needed to bring it back on track, and fast.

"When Con and I came back here after wasting the day looking at mug shots and learned about Del's run-in with the dog, we went straight to Joanna's clinic," he said. "I already knew about Alice's Skinwalker obsession, since she's asked me to visit her, too, and Joanna told me that the old lady had wanted to talk to Caro about it. That's when I left to go looking for her. But Skinwalker and Alice Tahe aren't important. What *is* important is that someone came close to killing you today, Caro, and since I don't buy your theory of a random speeder—"

"I don't buy it, either," she said promptly. "I wasn't thinking clearly immediately after the accident, but it's obvious to me now that Steve was deliberately attempting to—"

She stopped. He saw her eyes widen in excitement as she realized what she'd just said, and he heard an echo of the same tension in his voice as he prompted her.

"Dixon? You're saying he was the driver who ran you off the road?"

"But you didn't see his face," Del said. "Did you recognize his vehicle?"

"Not his vehicle, his ball cap," Caro said slowly. "Steve's hometown is Detroit. The driver was wearing a dark blue ball cap with a big white *D*. I don't know how often in the past I've seen Steve wearing it and heard Jess razzing him about being a die-hard Tigers fan."

"I hate to rain on anyone's parade, but a ball cap's not exactly conclusive evidence."

John MacLeish had been silent up until now. Since Gabe had learned that he and Daniel Bird weren't the type to talk unless they had something to say, Mac's comment got his attention. The ex–Beta Beta Force member shrugged apologetically.

"Especially when we have to assume that the driver who tried to kill Caro today was either Leo himself, or working for him. It's unlikely there's a second killer out there targeting her."

"Dixon can't be Leo," Gabe said flatly. "When the call came through from the man who called himself by that name, Steve was right there in the room with us. Besides, him being Leo would mean he'd arranged Jess's kidnapping for some unknown reason, and I can't buy that. He must have known his involvement would be in danger of being revealed as soon as Jess was released."

"But Jess wasn't released, he was killed," Caro pointed out. "His death warrant was signed when Steve gave Larry Kanin the go-ahead to barge in on a sensitive negotiation with guns blazing. Mac just said that if Ball Cap was Steve, then Steve has to be

Leo or working for Leo, but there's a possibility we've overlooked. What if *Leo's* working for *Steve?*''

He didn't like any of this, Gabe thought suddenly. He didn't like the way Caro was involving herself so wholeheartedly in this investigation, he didn't like her bandying around a theory that implied Jess's killer was someone close to her, and he didn't like the way she'd seemingly dismissed what had happened to her today. Del's assessment of her rescuer as a sicko was probably right: the man's behavior had been dangerously strange. But his presence on the scene had been all that had saved her from certain death.

The image that had flashed through his mind a dozen times in the past few hours seared across his imagination again—the rain-slick road, the blazing wreck coming into view, the terrible confirmation as he'd sped closer that the wreck was all that was left of the red four-by-four she'd been driving....

At that moment he'd known with absolute certainty that she was dead, and it had seemed to him as if the world had suddenly stopped spinning. A heartbeat later it had started up again when he'd seen her stumbling toward him from across the road.

*None of which means you're in love with the woman,* he told himself harshly. *Yeah, you fell for her, just a little, a long time ago. You even tried to convince yourself she'd fallen for you a little, too, until she made it damn clear she hadn't. Maybe there's something between you, on her side, as well as yours, but it doesn't involve hearts and flowers, Riggs. If you think just because she's wearing jeans she's not a snow princess anymore, you're heading for a second long fall where the lady's concerned.*

Which didn't change the fact that he'd taken on the job of keeping her and her baby safe. And if that meant playing the heavy, then that was what he'd have to do.

"Leo works for Steve Dixon." He didn't keep the skepticism from his tone. "Okay, let's run with that. Crawford Solutions' vice president somehow found his own tame criminal—we'll call him Leo, to keep this simple—and not only does Dixon give the orders to Leo, he trusts Leo won't double-cross him and keep the ransom himself. Have I got it right?"

"Not quite," Caro said crisply. Blue eyes blazed at him from across the table. "Leo's no criminal, he's a puppet, coached by Steve on what to say during the phone calls so Steve would have exactly the alibi you just gave him—that he was in the room when the kidnapper called."

"You're forgetting the scrambling device and the voice filter. You're talking hard-core contraband, not something jerry-rigged out of components bought from a mall electronics store. Even if Dixon had the contacts to hire the thugs he sent to the handover, there's no way he would have known who to go to for equipment like that."

He stood. "Your theory's as improbable as Alice Tahe's Skinwalker scenario, princess. Why don't you leave the—"

"Dixon couldn't jerry-rig those things, no." She returned his gaze. "But I know someone who could...and that someone would have *jumped* at the chance to get back at Jess.''

He knew why he didn't like any of this, Gabe realized. He'd known from the moment she'd walked into the kitchen, but he hadn't wanted to own up to his reasons.

*Because those reasons don't paint you in a real good light, do they, buddy? She needed you. If history's anything to go by, she would have dumped you as soon as she'd gotten what she wanted from you, but for now she needed you—to handle the situation, to protect her, to keep Emily safe. This new Caro might just be tough enough not to need a burned-out case like Gabe Riggs.*

And that was his problem, not hers.

He met her gaze. ''Disgruntled computer genius, hired by Dixon and fired by Jess, then given an opportunity to hit back at his ex-boss—an opportunity he might not have realized included murder. Are you thinking of the same someone I'm thinking of?''

''Andrew Scott,'' Caro said. ''Except—''

He nodded. ''Except, I didn't investigate him when I first heard he'd disappeared. And now Scott's probably sunk out of sight, thanks to my screwup.''

## Chapter Nine

"Huge mistake," Caro muttered under her breath as she padded down the hall in the dark and descended the shadowy stairs. "Huge, *huge* mistake. What was I thinking, letting Susannah take Emily for the night?"

That question was easily answered, she admitted. When the after-dinner discussion had ended with Connor suggesting he use his former FBI contacts to locate Scott, and Gabe curtly informing the group that he would use some ex–Recoveries International comrades to post a twenty-four/seven watch on Steve Dixon in case the Crawford Solutions' vice president intended to bolt, Susannah had drawn her aside.

"Tess and I figure it'd do you a world of good to have a night by yourself, Caro," she'd said, her soft West Virginia drawl uncharacteristically firm. "Being a mama myself and knowing how I fret when baby Danny's not with me, I guess you're goin' to tell me you don't need a girls' night in, with nothing to do but relax. But I won't take no for an answer. While Tye's down in Mexico liasing with those *federale* police, me and Danny have been stayin' with Tess and

Con and their rapscallion, Joey, so one more little one won't be a problem. And you've been through the wringer today.''

It had been a generous and warmhearted offer, Caro thought now. She'd accepted—mostly because she'd worried that after the events of the day she would be out like a light as soon as her head hit the pillow and might not hear Emily if her baby daughter woke up in the night.

''Out like a light,'' she snorted softly now as she felt her way through the kitchen in the dark and grasped the refrigerator door handle. ''*Wired* like a light's more like it. I'm buzzing so much from that coffee I had after supper I doubt even a glass of milk's going to—''

The glow from the opened refrigerator illuminated the room. Out of the corner of her eye Caro saw a man sitting at the kitchen table, and she bit back a squeak.

*So much for your new tough image,* she thought. Chagrin lent a note of testiness to her voice as she plunked the carton of milk on the table and fixed Gabe with a stare.

''You really have to stop giving me heart attacks in the middle of the night, Riggs,'' she told him. She nodded at the partially open door leading off the kitchen. ''Your bedroom's right there. Why come out here to sit in the dark?''

As she spoke she flicked on the light and got a momentary glimpse of a bare chest and well-worn jeans riding low on lean hips. Gabe tipped back his chair, reached behind him and flicked it off again.

"It's not dark, your eyes just haven't adjusted yet. I could ask you the same question. What are you doing, wandering around the house in the small hours in your underwear?"

"Hardly my underwear." She raised an eyebrow at him. "Shortie pj's, and they cover everything they're supposed to. I couldn't sleep. What's your excuse?"

He was right, it wasn't completely dark, she realized as she got a glass from the cupboard and sat down at the table. A small light burned at the porch entrance just past the screen door.

"I was going over my options."

She glanced at him through her lashes. "Options? Have you changed your mind about putting a surveillance team on the Lazy J to watch Steve?"

He shook his head. "I made the calls while you were getting Emily ready for Susannah. The team's already in place, although I doubt Dixon will do anything to draw attention to himself right now. My guess is, he plans to wait until the initial excitement over Jess's kidnapping and death subsides, quietly resign from Crawford Solutions with some excuse like his heart just isn't in it anymore, and then just as quietly disappear. That would be the smart way to do it."

He frowned. "Although I could be giving him too much credit. Trying to eliminate you today wasn't the action of a man who's thinking clearly."

"It was the action of a man who was desperate," she agreed. "The question is, why would *I* make

Dixon feel desperate—so desperate he took the risk of trying to kill me himself?''

''It wasn't such a risk. It was never a secret that you'd gone to the Double B and that the Double B was where we were concentrating our protection. He had nothing to lose by keeping an eye on the place on the off chance you might give him an opportunity to get you alone.''

''Which I did. Like Mac pointed out, one quick glimpse of a ball cap isn't evidence enough for the authorities to take Steve in for questioning, and now he's going to be watching his step. My little expedition to see Alice Tahe made your job a whole lot harder, didn't it.''

''It gave us something to go on, which was more than we had before. Tomorrow we'll have you set up with a computer and modem, and you can use the password Jess provided you with when he gave you power of attorney to start looking into the Crawford Solutions' accounts. Maybe we'll find an answer there to the question of why Dixon wanted you out of the way.''

Abruptly he shoved his chair back. ''Wrong pronoun. Maybe *you'll* find an answer. The option I'm considering is bowing out of this investigation and handing over the reins to Connor.''

By now her eyes had adjusted completely. Caro stared at him, taking in the rigid set of his jaw, the careful lack of expression on his face.

''You can't.'' She heard the sharpness in her voice, but dismay made it impossible to soften her tone. ''Damn it, Gabe, I won't *let* you.''

''That's the Caro Moore I'm used to.'' His observation was edged. ''Look, princess, I told you when you came to me that Jess didn't deserve to have a has-been handling his abduction, and I've proved that all the way down the line. I let him get killed. I didn't pick up on the Andrew Scott thing. And for a minute today, I was certain that my incompetence had cost you your life.''

''You had no reason to suspect Scott before now,'' she argued. ''And I was in danger today only through my own recklessness, as I've already admitted. You told me not to leave the Double B, Gabe. I didn't listen.''

''Yeah, but I should have known you wouldn't listen.'' He stood. ''Let's stop beating around the bush, sweetheart. You and I have a history. We slept together. That should have disqualified me from taking on this assignment, but instead I tried to tell myself I'd be able to be objective where you were concerned. For some reason, I've found I can't be. You have every right to want to be part of the investigation, and just hearing you discuss the case drives me crazy. No wonder you seized the opportunity to jaunt off by yourself this afternoon and get out from under the cotton wool I've tried to wrap you in since you got here.''

Caro realized her mouth was open. She closed it with a snap. It had all seemed so crystal-clear when she had believed she only had minutes to live. She'd wished for just this opportunity to tell Gabe how she felt, but now that she had it, the words wouldn't come.

*"We slept together."* That was all their night eighteen months ago had meant to him, a less-than-meaningful history that was inconveniently preventing him from keeping this on a strictly businesslike level. Once she would have masked the pain of that revelation with a coolly cutting remark.

*But I'm not the snow princess anymore,* she told herself with a flash of anger. *And I've had just about enough of Gabriel Riggs's dismissal of what happened between him and me as a mistake he wishes he could take back.*

Because, whether he knew it or not, he didn't want to take it back. He didn't love her. He wasn't going to be there for her in the future. But what she'd told him the day she'd caught up with him in the desert still held true—he'd been marked by the night they'd had, and he would bear those marks for a long, long time.

He wanted her. If she couldn't have anything else from him, she was going to force him to face up to that, at least.

"For heaven's sake, Gabe, none of that's a reason to take yourself off this case. We both know why you can't be objective about me. Maybe if you admitted a few home truths to yourself, we could start working together to find—"

"A few home truths?" His narrowed gaze followed her as she got up from the table and set her glass in the sink. "What are you talking about?"

"The same thing I was talking about the last time you were snapping at me one minute and kissing me the next," she said impatiently, "the day I tracked you down to that dump of a gas station you were living in. You promised me that when I came to you the third time you'd have the strength of character to turn me down, but then you promptly followed up that impressive-sounding speech with a kiss that was anything but detached.''

She planted her hands on her hips. ''You've got the hots for me, Gabriel. You've had them since you first laid eyes on me. That's why you can't think straight and that's why you can't treat me like a partner in this, so why won't you admit it?''

He took in a breath, his eyes never leaving hers. ''You've really decided to kick over the traces, haven't you, sweetheart?'' he said softly. ''That's pretty tough talk, coming from a woman who once accused me of planning a seduction when I told her I didn't want to risk our lives by driving through a blizzard.''

''I hope you didn't get too attached to that woman.'' She tipped her head at him. ''Because I don't really miss her.''

''I can see that.'' A muscle moved in his jaw. ''Okay, since the new Caro Moore wants it given to her straight, here goes. Maybe I do have the hots for you, honey—your phrase, not mine. Maybe during my stay in the desert I hit the replay button a couple of hundred times on the memory of that night we had, and maybe when you walked into the kitchen earlier this evening I took one look at you and had the insane impulse to hustle you into my bed. I'm not going to. Want to know why?''

Why didn't hearing him admit he wanted her take

any of the pain away? Caro wondered with a frown. After all, it meant there was one tiny chink in his armor where she was concerned, one area where he had no defense against her, didn't it?

But the confession he'd just made wasn't the one she'd wanted to hear at all, she realized with sudden clarity.

*You want him to tell you he loves you. You want him to tell you he's not going anywhere, that leaving you would tear him apart, that he's ready to put down those roots Del was talking about. You want permanence and commitment from the man—and since he's never been able to find those things for himself, there's no way he can give them to you and his daughter.*

The smile she gave him felt pasted on. "I can guess why. It's got something to do with the way it ended so badly between us last time, right? It's got something to do with you feeling your past involvement with me is distracting you from this job. I told you, Gabe, I've changed. The woman I am now is pretty savvy about the way the world works. She doesn't need things spelled out for her."

"Good for her," he said tersely. "She still doesn't know the first thing about the man I am."

Faint anger overlaid some of her unhappiness. "I know I was just a one-night stand for you. You said it a moment ago—we slept together, that's all. The morning after we did, you couldn't wait to see the last of me."

He stared at her, the gleam from the porch light outside accentuating the hard ridge of his cheekbones.

"The morning after, you couldn't wait to remind me of the ground rules, princess. The morning after, you asked me to promise to stick to them. It never happened, I wouldn't call you, and you didn't have to worry about running into me again, remember?" His jaw tightened. "Why let myself think of it as anything more than a one-night stand, when that's all it was for you?"

The last of Caro's composure fled. "That's all it ever could have been for me, since when I tried to find you a few weeks later you'd dropped off the face of the earth. Damn you, Riggs—you served a year at the Double B when you were a teen, so you've obviously broken the rules once or twice in your life! Why did you have to take them so seriously *this* time?"

Dark brows drew together in a scowl. He took a step toward her, the pulse at the side of his neck noticeable even in the dim light. "Are you saying you wish I hadn't?"

Too late she saw the opening she'd given him. She tried to bolster her defenses with a shrug. "What kind of question is that?"

He was close enough that she heard his indrawn breath. The thick brush of his lashes obscured whatever expression was in his eyes. "I'll ask you again, honey. Are you saying you wish I hadn't kept to your damn rules?"

"For heaven's sake." Suddenly finding it impossible to keep up eye contact, Caro looked away, the words coming from her in a rush. "If you must know, yes. Yes, I wish you hadn't kept to them, yes, I wish

I'd never come up with the stupid things in the first place, yes, yes, *yes*. Are you happy now?''

''Delirious, sweetheart.''

His growl came from far back in his throat. The next moment his outspread hands were on either side of her face, and she found herself forced to meet his gaze.

''Tell me one last thing.'' He ground out the words. ''Why do you make me work so hard for everything, Caro?''

A final spurt of defiance rose in her. ''Because I can, Gabe,'' she snapped. ''Why do you do the same to me?''

''Oh, hell, princess. Probably because I can, too,'' he muttered, bringing his mouth down on hers.

In the split second that he did, there was just enough time for Caro to reassure herself. She knew how Gabe Riggs kissed, she thought swiftly. Summer lightning. Sparks. Bright heat running immediately through her. She was ready for him, wasn't she?

She wasn't ready at all.

Suddenly she wasn't in the kitchen of the Double B, she was falling through a moonless sky toward an invisible ocean. She felt herself slipping beneath the black surface, felt herself plunging endlessly, the water wrapping like ink-dipped silk between and around her legs, her arms, her body.

There was no summer lightning. There was no light at all. There was just an onrush of darkly urgent desire.

Gabe's tongue went deeper. His hands moved down her neck, her arms, to her hips. Through the worn denim of his jeans she felt him harden against her as he grasped the lace-trimmed hems of her pyjama shorts and hiked them upward, his fingers spreading tautly wide on her exposed skin.

A shiver ran all the way from her heels up to her inner thighs and back down again, as if a feather were skimming lightly over her. Arching against him, Caro let her own fingertips curl against the muscled wall of his chest, and pressed her nails lightly into his skin.

"Don't start what you can't finish, honey," he rasped, lifting his mouth from hers enough to mutter the warning against her lips. "If we go through with this it's on the understanding that tomorrow no one gets to pretend it didn't happen. If you can't handle that, tell me now."

"If I can't handle it?" Caro murmured back. "Don't worry about me, Gabe, worry about yourself."

She didn't know where the reckless words had come from, she thought a split-second later. Or maybe she did. They'd come from the woman she'd seen in the mirror earlier this evening, the woman who'd looked tough and competent and edgy. That woman might have wanted hearts and flowers from Gabe, too, but she wasn't going to let the lack of them stand in the way of taking whatever the man had to give.

He wasn't offering forever. But he'd made it clear that this was more than just a one-night stand, as far as he was concerned. For a dyed-in-the-wool loner like Gabe Riggs, that was probably the nearest he could get to commitment.

And for the woman in the mirror—for *me,* Caro

thought defiantly—it was the nearest she'd ever get to what she really wanted from him.

*One day you'll walk out of my life again, Gabriel,* she told him silently. *But you'll never be able to forget me completely. I'm going to make sure of that tonight.*

"Worry about myself?" There was startled humor in his eyes. "Princess, I can handle anything you can dish out, and then some. I'll admit you rocked my world the last time we—"

"I didn't just rock your world, Riggs, I hit a 9.5 on the Richter scale," Caro retorted. "This time I intend to bring you to your knees. Want to back out while you still can?"

A grin ghosted across his hard features. "So that's how it's going to be, is it? It's payback time for every stupid thing I said at the gas station the day you tracked me down, right?"

"Not for everything you said," she informed him. "Just the part about me never having had to say please for anything in my life, and how one day you were going to hear that word from me." She shook her head decisively. "Go ahead and give it your best shot, but I think you're the one who's going to end up saying 'pretty please' tonight, Riggs."

Had this scandalous new Caro always been lurking just beneath the porcelain facade of the woman she'd once been? Caro wondered in brief incredulity. She had to have been, because the teasing dare she'd just flung at Gabe had come from her without any effort at all.

And the molten amber in his gaze as he took in her challenge was touching off an answering heat in her.

"You're on, lady."

His growl was hoarser than normal. Brushing past him to the partially open door of his bedroom, impulsively Caro hooked a finger into the waistband of his jeans and gave a tug.

"Then, what are you waiting for?" she said, lowering her own tone to huskiness.

Unlike her room upstairs, the first-floor spare bedroom of the Double B was definitely a man's sleeping quarters, she saw as she entered. A double bed and a small bedside table with a shaded lamp on it took up most of one wall, an unmirrored dresser much of another, and the third was obviously windows, judging from the jute curtains pulled across its length. An oval rag rug provided the only touch of color, since the neatly turned-down sheets and accompanying blanket on the bed were plain white and army green, respectively.

*Definitely* a man's room, Caro thought, her confidence suddenly slipping in reaction to the starkness of her surroundings. In fact, the only out-of-place femininity in it was herself.

"I didn't give you a romantic setting last time, either, as I recall." She turned to see Gabe's lips curve wryly as he took in her unguarded expression. "A borrowed chalet, your own fur coat on the floor and a blizzard raging outside."

"It doesn't matter," she began, but he shook his head decisively.

"Yeah, it matters. Close your eyes."

The man was a master at keeping her off balance, Caro thought as she dubiously complied. The last thing she would have guessed he was thinking about right now was romance. If she weren't careful, she might fool herself into believing him capable of giving her those hearts and flowers she secretly yearned for from him, and that would be a mistake.

"You can look now."

All he'd done was to turn out the bedside lamp and part the curtains, she thought in confusion as she blinked against the darkness. She felt his hand grip hers and draw her closer to the opened window.

"Dineh diamonds, princess." There was a wry note in his voice. "I've seen you throw the other kind away, but I figured even a poor little rich girl like you might be impressed if I surrounded you with these."

As he spoke he nodded at the night sky outside. Following his gaze, Caro felt her breath catch in her throat.

The sky was black velvet, strewn with more stars than she'd ever seen in her life. They twinkled like the diamonds he'd compared them to, and even as she watched she saw one shoot across the sky, followed closely by another. Silently she made two wishes, and then she turned her face to him.

"They're beautiful, Gabe," she breathed. "Did you order them up just for me?"

"Damn straight, honey," he agreed. "I thought they'd take the edge off Del's Marine Corps decor a little if you happened to wander in here for any reason tonight."

His tone was light, and she made an effort to match

it. "Was there anything else you had planned for if I happened to wander in here?"

"One or two possibilities came to mind," he murmured. "Should I run them by you to see if you approve?"

"You'd better." Thoughtfully she bit her lip. "You know how we ex–rich bitches can be, and you don't even have a snowbank handy to throw me into."

"Good point." A corner of his mouth quirked upward, but his shadowed gaze held hers intently. "Okay, how's this? Since you stripped off a sweater for me last time, how about if I return the favor for you now?"

As he spoke his hands moved to the buttoned fly of his jeans. Caro's mouth was suddenly so dry she found it hard to speak.

"No way, Riggs," she said, putting his hands aside and slipping the first button free. "I was planning to do that."

"And you're the boss?"

"Something like that," she answered unevenly, working on the second button and releasing it, as well.

Starlight gleamed on the washboard ripples of his abs and overlaid the coppery tan of his skin with pale silver, but although shadows darkened the opened vee of his jeans, Caro could feel Gabe's growing response to her actions by the strained tautness of the denim. She fumbled a third button free, and heard his sudden intake of breath.

"Princess, I'm begging you," he rasped. "If I'm going to be any use to you at all, you're going to have to switch your attention to some other area for a while. I'm not made of stone.''

The rawness in his voice was borne out by the tightness of his grip as he firmly removed her hands. Disconcerted, she glanced up at his face.

His mouth was a grim line. His lashes, thick and dark, obscured the obsidian of his eyes. Even as she looked she saw him drag in another tight breath and release it carefully.

He was the very picture of a man on the edge. And he'd been brought to the edge by her. The realization came to her, hot and sweet and overpoweringly erotic.

The man in front of her had spent most of his life in situations where only his rigid self-control had stood between him and disaster. That accounted for his seeming lack of emotion at times, his air of unassailable self-sufficiency. Long ago Gabe Riggs had learned not to give himself over to a particular moment, a particular sensation, a particular woman. But somehow with her he forgot those hard-won lessons.

It didn't change the fact that whatever they had would be temporary…it just made it possible for her to forget that fact for a while.

''I'm not made of stone, either, Gabe,'' she said. ''We've got a night ahead of us to tease each other, but right now I don't think I can wait another minute to have you. I—I want to see what those diamonds look like when I'm lying in your bed and you're making—''

The heavy muscles of his arms flexing as he pulled her to him, Gabe didn't give her a chance to finish. ''God help me, but I don't think I can wait, either,'' he said huskily, his hands slipping under her lace-trimmed top and encircling her waist. "Like I said, in the desert I replayed our one night together over and over again in my mind, but it never came close to the real thing, and I knew it. I need the real thing again. I need to feel you under me and on top of me, and I need you touching me everywhere I remember you touching me before."

This time his kiss was slow and deep, and at some point during it, Caro dimly realized he'd lifted her completely off her feet. Her arms twined around his neck as she felt him lower her to the bed.

"You wanted to see what the stars looked like from here. I want to see what they look like shining down on you," he murmured, deftly undoing the few tiny buttons that marched down the front of her top.

The next moment his head bent to her, and a wave of pure pleasure washed over her as the tip of his tongue flicked against the peak of first one breast, and then the other. Sensation mounted as his palms encompassed her and his thumbs traced soft twin curves, but it wasn't until she felt the heat of his mouth burning a line past her rib cage, her stomach, to the tops of her thighs, that Caro felt herself losing control.

He was the only man who'd ever done this to her, she thought dizzily. He was the only man she ever *wanted* doing this to her. He seemed to know unerringly just how much exquisite torment she could take before giving her the briefest of reprieves, and then bringing her even closer to the edge the next time.

"Please, Gabe," she managed to say breathlessly. "Please, it's—"

All possibility of rational speech disappeared as the heat that had been building in her suddenly burst into searingly consuming flames. A series of convulsive shudders ran through her, and even as they did she heard Gabe's hoarse whisper against her ear, felt his palms smoothing back her hair.

"I love it when you melt, snow princess." There was a ragged edge to his tone, and even in her dazed state she understood that he'd come almost as close to losing himself as she had. "Tell me you like it, too."

"I—I love it, Gabe." A final shudder turned her sentence to a sigh, and she pressed herself closer to him, feeling the hard evidence of his own unfulfilled need against her. "I love it so much I want it all over again," she murmured, sliding her hands lightly down to the last secured button on his jeans. "Except this time I want you with me all the way."

*All the way, and over and over again,* Caro thought as she watched Gabe step out of his jeans a few minutes later and turn to her, the familiar turquoise and silver cuff on his left wrist all the more striking because it was the only thing he was wearing.

*Right up until dawn takes our diamonds from the sky, Gabe. That's what I wished on the first shooting star, and it looks like that wish is about to come true. But my second wish was even more important. Maybe someday I'll be able to tell you what it—*

Gabe's mouth came down on hers. Forgetting everything else, Caro gave herself up to the man and the night and the desire flaming through her.

## Chapter Ten

"Sometimes I'm glad I never learned to use computers."

Del's wife, Greta, elegant even in a pair of paint-smeared jeans and with her hair bound into a braid, strolled into the bookshelf-lined room. Caro, sitting at the oak library table, computer monitor and keyboard in front of her and Emma napping in a carry-cot on the floor beside her, gave a weary smile.

"Right now I wish I'd never learned, either, believe me."

Greta's laugh was easy. "You need a break. John MacLeish and Daniel are still out checking the perimeter fence for repairs with Gabe, and Del's watching the house and the yard from the lookout post by the barn, so I set a pitcher of iced tea on the porch for us girls. I'm just dying to plop Miss Cutie-Pie on my lap and hold her for a while anyway."

Miss Cutie-Pie had to be Emma, Caro surmised with a grin. Greta had fallen head over heels in love with her, and had eagerly volunteered her baby-sitting services over the past two days while Caro had been poring over the Crawford Solutions' finances on the computer that had been provided for her. She got to her feet and rubbed her derriere.

"A break's definitely called for," she agreed.

"Oh, how adorable!"

Greta's exclamation came as Caro lifted the cot onto the library table—the table, she'd learned from Gabe, where he and the rest of the Double B bad boys had labored over homework during their stints at the ranch years ago. It had made her feel better to know she wasn't the only one to spend interminable hours here, she'd informed him this morning when he'd looked in to see how she was progressing, but if he really wanted to ease her boredom she could think of better ways he could accomplish that.

Warmth touched her cheeks at the memory of how he'd taken her suggestions under consideration, and swiftly she switched her attention back to Greta, who was delightedly examining the minute moccasins encasing Emma's tiny kicking feet.

"Where'd you find such small ones?"

Greta carefully lifted Emma from the cot, and when little fingers grabbed at her long braid, the artist's cat-green eyes widened.

Caro's heart sunk at the assessing glance Greta gave the delicate silver and turquoise bracelet around Emma's wrist, and sunk further as that green gaze dwelt for a moment on her.

"Gabe's a big softie when it comes to little girls, I guess," she ventured weakly. "He bought the bracelet and the moccasins for Emma yesterday when he visited the Dinetah to talk to Joanna Tahe's Tribal

Police brother, Matt, about the attack on me the day before.''

''The Tribal Police haven't gotten a lead on either the driver of the truck who ran you off the road or the man who pulled you from the wreckage?'' Greta frowned as they made their way onto the porch and she settled into one of the rustic pine chairs, Emma on her lap.

Caro shook her head while pouring them both glasses of iced tea from the pitcher on the low table between the chairs. Her own glass in her hand, she leaned back against the porch railing. ''No. That's why Con's in Albuquerque today, trying to persuade the FBI to take a more active part in the investigation. If I'm right and Ball Cap is Steve, he made it on and off the Dinetah without being noticed. By the time the Recoveries International men that Gabe contacted got into surveillance position around the Lazy J, he was already back there, if he'd ever left in the first place. As for my weirdo rescuer, Matt told Gabe he didn't leave so much as a footprint in the mud.''

''The rain didn't help,'' Greta said. ''Some of the Tribal Police are incredible trackers, but they can't perform miracles. So now what?''

''So now I just keep looking for a needle in a haystack.'' Caro grimaced. ''To make things worse, the needle might not even be in this particular haystack.''

''You mean, if you were wrong about Steve Dixon being the man who ran you off the road and you're going through Crawford Solutions' financial records looking for some indication that he's been bilking the company, when he could be totally innocent,'' the other woman declared. She gave a thoughtful nod. "That's a possibility. But as an artist I run into that same problem all the time."

She smiled down at the little girl in her arms before meeting Caro's puzzled gaze. "The way I see it, when I stand in front of a blank canvas, everything's already there, just waiting to be revealed," she explained. "I make an attempt to bring that hidden picture out, but I usually don't get it right the first time, so I scrape off the paint and start from scratch again."

"Frustrating," Caro said glumly.

Greta shook her head. "Not really. Because every time I start over again, I know I'm getting closer to the truth I'm trying to uncover. That's how you have to look at this Steve Dixon lead. If you eventually come to the conclusion that there's absolutely no evidence he had a motive to get rid of Jess, then we can start concentrating on someone else, like the computer genius who disappeared before Jess's Mexico trip."

"Andrew Scott." Caro drained her glass and set it on the table. "I see your point, but I still wish the FBI hadn't drawn the line at assigning their forensic accountants to this. Those people are trained to spot discrepancies in company books. I'm not."

Greta shrugged. "As Connor said, since the crime took place in Mexico, the Bureau's worried the *federales* might see anything more than peripheral involvement as a breach of jurisdiction. When Con spoke to his Bureau contact yesterday, he got the impression he was pushing it by requesting an APB be put out on Andrew Scott."

"And of course we can't hire outside accountants,'' Caro sighed. ''I have a duty to the company not to create the kind of panic that would bring about, if it ever got out.''

''Although not a duty to stockholders, since Crawford Solutions never went public,'' Greta noted. ''Do you know who inherits, Caro?''

''I don't have a clue.'' She gave a wry smile. ''Jess probably left everything to the Flat Earth Society, or whatever his latest enthusiasm was.'' Her smile faded. ''I hate to say it, but that's another reason why it's important that his body's found. Until it is, he can't legally be declared dead and his estate's in limbo. I— I hope Tye has news for us soon,'' she ended unhappily.

''I do, too. Del won't feel right until Jess's body is properly laid to rest beside his mother's in the Crawford plot. He sees that as a final fulfillment of an old responsibility, I suppose,'' Greta said quietly.

''Del knew Jess's mom, Sheila, right?'' Caro wrinkled her brow. ''Jess mentioned that he did, but I never knew the details.''

''Sheila Crawford grew up in the same town as my old mustang—'' Greta smiled ''—although from the little I've gathered, back then Del was more of a young stallion. Captain of his high-school football team, a smooth dancer, had his own souped-up jalopy. He's still a babe as far as this girl's concerned, but at eighteen he must have been a heartbreaker. Sheila was only a junior at the time, and I suspect she idolized him. When he was sent to 'Nam, she wrote him on a regular basis.''

She caught Caro's quizzical glance. ''Oh, not love

letters. Del told me Sheila's letters were like getting news of home from a sister. I think they were all that kept him going sometimes, which is why he always had a soft spot for her—a soft spot that grew to include her son, since Jess's father was never in the picture.''

Greta's lips pressed together. ''Del was one of the few who knew Sheila's pregnancy was the result of a rape, although the incident was so traumatic that she never told Jess himself. That was another reason why Del took the boy in for a year when he got into trouble over a computer-hacking incident at school and Sheila felt he needed a firmer hand than she could provide. Jess was the only bad boy who wasn't sent here by the authorities,'' she added with a small smile, ''unlike a certain hot-wirer of cars I could name who seems to have recently put his past completely behind him.''

There was a teasing note in her voice as she reverted back to their earlier subject. ''A big softie when it comes to little girls? More like a big softie when it comes to little girls and their mamas. Gabe's been a different man these last two days, and judging from the smoldering glances you and he have been giving each other when you think no one's watching, the reason why isn't too hard to figure out.''

As Caro sat in front of the computer monitor half an hour later, Gabe's words from two nights ago ran through her mind for about the thousandth time since he'd uttered them. *''Tomorrow no one gets to pretend it didn't happen…''* Greta was right, she thought with a blush—even the most casual observer had only to glance at the two of them together to know the exact nature of their relationship. Little things gave them away, she thought—little things like the way his gaze immediately sought hers when she walked into a room, the way she couldn't seem to stop smiling whenever he was around, the way both of them apparently found it necessary to touch each other's hand to make the most mundane of points during a discussion.

And of course, if that casual onlooker should ever happen to walk in on them when they were alone…

Caro tried to concentrate on the information on the monitor in front of her, but it was no use. Instant heat rose in her. He hadn't argued that first morning when she'd insisted on returning to her own bed before the household awakened, but on the two mornings since, he'd made it clear he didn't intend to hide the fact that he was no longer sleeping in the downstairs guest room.

"Skulking isn't my style." His growl had lacked its former edge, maybe because of the grin quirking up a corner of his mouth. "Besides, we're all adults here. If Del should happen to walk out of his and Greta's bedroom at the same time I come out of yours, I don't think he'll be exactly shocked."

He hadn't used the word *love.* He hadn't alluded to the possibility of any kind of a future with her once Jess's killer had been captured. Maybe she was reading way more into their relationship than Gabe intended.

*Which is why I haven't told him Emily's his,* she thought with a pang. *And until I know for sure that he feels the same way I do, I can't risk telling him. He adores her, that's obvious. But having a father who showers her with presents when he shows up once every six months and then goes off to live his own life the rest of the year isn't what I want for my little girl. Emily deserves a father who's there for her all the time, not a sexy loner who shares her mom's bed on a part-time basis.*

And right now, Caro reminded herself with a sigh, Emily deserved a mother who was able to concentrate on the matter at hand. With an effort she shut out her worries and hopes about Gabe and forced herself to focus on the columns of figures on the screen.

"Same old, same old," she muttered. "$X$ amount of dollars for one expense, $Y$ amount for another, except these outlays are for the construction of the new plant in Mexico. Architect's fees, contracting, materials…"

She lifted her shoulders in frustration. Even if Steve had been diverting monies meant for the new plant to himself under a false company name, how would she know? Milagro Construction could be a legitimate firm, or it could be the cover alias for a Swiss bank account. Same with the rest of the companies—Diego Truss and Roofing, Sandoval Concrete—

She froze, her stunned gaze fixed on a familiar name buried halfway down the list. Then she almost jumped out of her chair as a hand dropped lightly onto her shoulder.

"I know, I know. I have to stop giving you heart attacks." As she looked up to meet Gabe's rueful smile, he went on contritely, "Sorry, I didn't mean to startle you. I met Del and Greta outside and told Del I'd take over guard duty on the house if he wanted to check out the wolf tracks I saw while I was mending the perimeter fence with Mac and Daniel. Greta went with him, so for once we've got the place to ourselves.'' He grinned. ''Well, except for Emily. Where is she?''

''Upstairs having a nap,'' Caro said numbly. ''Gabe, I—''

But already he was frowning and drawing her to her feet. ''You look like you've seen a ghost. What's the matter?''

''You've hit the nail right on the head,'' she answered, her voice muffled against his chest as he held her. Pulling slightly away, she dipped her head toward the monitor. ''I have seen a ghost, Gabe…the same ghost that's materialized before in this case. Take a look at the name of that electrical supply firm—it's the largest payout on the screen.''

Frowning, he put her from him and drew closer to the monitor. Under his chambray shirt, his shoulders tensed at the same time as she heard his quickly indrawn breath.

''Dos Abejas Electronics Company,'' Caro said, the momentary unevenness gone from her voice, leaving it steady and cold. ''Two Bees, as in Bravo Bravo, as in the name on the side of the truck where Jess was killed, as in the Double B. As I say, Gabe, either a ghost from the past is back and walking again, or—'' She paused and met his eyes.

''Or someone's going to a hell of a lot of trouble to make us think so,'' he finished grimly for her.

"You know, honey, I think it's time we had ourselves a little talk with Mr. Steve Dixon."

"ABDUCTION. ASSAULT. Terror tactics, for God's sake!"

One of the men flanking the Crawford vice president in the kitchen of the Double B raised an eyebrow at this last, but remained silent as Dixon went on, his voice climbing even higher.

"Not to mention that your thugs have apparently been staked out around the Lazy J to watch my comings and goings over the past few days, Riggs. When I'm finished with you, you won't be allowed to negotiate the release of a stray dog from the city pound, damn you!"

"We handled him with kid gloves, just like you said to, Gabe." The speaker was one of the men standing beside Dixon. "Told him he had the choice of being escorted here to answer some questions about monies diverted from his late boss's pocket to his or having us take him to the nearest police station to be charged with embezzlement, for starters. I'm not real sure where the terror tactics came in."

"He wanted time to change his clothes and make a few phone calls," the second man flanking Dixon said laconically. "We advised him that wasn't in the game plan. Maybe that was it."

The two former Recoveries International operatives were about Gabe's age, Caro surmised, and like him, they had an air of tense alertness about them. Their work boots and tan work shirts with photo IDs clipped to the breast pockets jibed with Gabe's information that they'd been posing as telephone linemen working the stretch of road by the Lazy J. Although their dust-begrimed attire was no more polished than Dixon's untucked shirt and baggy walking shorts, the executive's outfit seemed foolishly casual in comparison.

That casualness extended to the Detroit Tigers ball cap jammed backward on Steve's head.

Looking at him now, she thought it hardly seemed possible that he'd been the instigating force behind Jess's kidnapping and murder and also the faceless assailant who'd run her off the road only days ago. But the proof was in front of her on the kitchen table, in the form of a printout of the pertinent sections of Crawford Solutions' accounts showing transfers of staggering sums to a company that didn't exist, as a quick call to Gabe's *federale* contact, Captain Estavez, had confirmed.

The transfers had been authorized by Dixon. Although any prosecutor hoping to convict him would need to tie the dummy company's Swiss bank account to him, Gabe had informed her while they'd been waiting for the vice president's arrival, that that wouldn't pose an insurmountable problem.

"The bad press the Swiss banks recently got when their long-ago involvement with Nazi moneymen came to light put pressure on them to cooperate a little more fully with international law enforcement agencies," he'd said with grim satisfaction. "That cooperation widened when they realized the free world wouldn't stand for terrorists' war funds being protected by shields of secrecy. It'll take time and a court order, but in the end the boys in Zurich will wash their hands of client number 527242927."

His mouth had tightened. "Yeah, it didn't escape my notice that there were an awful lot of two's in that number, princess. But since Dixon wouldn't have been able to choose it, we'll have to write that one off as coincidence and not as a reference to double bees or two bees or anything like that. The other instances, though…"

"The other instances were a deliberate smoke-screen on his part." Caro had heard the thread of anger in her own voice and hadn't tried to modulate it. "Although Jess never mentioned Del's Beta Beta Force history to me, he must have let something slip to Steve. He wouldn't have seen any reason not to. Steve obviously saw this Double B angle as a perfect red herring."

"So he has his hired cutthroats steal a truck with that particular logo on it?" Gabe didn't sound entirely convinced.

"Or maybe he saw the truck on one of his visits to check on the construction of the site, and that gave him the idea to use the Double B smokescreen." Caro shook her head. "From what Tye's reported to you, the fruit company was a local firm, so it could have happened that way. The main thing is, he wanted to divert suspicion away from himself, so he planted those veiled references to Beta Beta Force right from the start."

"Leo's 'Bravo, Mr. Riggs, bravo,'" Gabe said tightly. "Leo being Dixon's mouthpiece and parroting the words Dixon told him to say."

"And Leo probably being Andrew Scott," Caro had agreed. "It was a stroke of genius to stage a murder as a kidnapping gone wrong, Gabe—evil genius, but still genius. Jess—" she faltered but went on "—Jess was always supposed to die on that road. With the events at the Double B that had been occupying his attention behind him, I know he was trying to get back up to speed on the Crawford Solutions' developments he'd let slide. Those included the Mexico plant, and Steve must have known that as soon as Jess began taking a more hands-on approach, like actually visiting the site itself to check on its progress, there was a possibility he'd discover he was being scammed."

She'd met his gaze. "You've been blaming yourself for his death, but it was no more your fault than Roswell's was. If Larry Kanin and his men hadn't charged in there with guns blazing, the shooting would have started some other way. That *had* to be how Dixon planned it—his orders to those thugs would have been to get the money and then stage some kind of flare-up that ended in Jess being killed."

She hoped she'd convinced him, Caro thought now, taking in the rigid set of Gabe's shoulders and the carved implacability of his features as he shoved the printout across the table to a still-protesting Steve. His guilt over Jess's death was all the more destructive because he thought of the Double B as home, and those he'd spent time here with as his family.

*Not that he'd ever admit it, which is a whole different problem,* she told herself as Steve ran a finger down the lines of figures and then turned to the next page of the printout. *Del's right—Gabe does need roots. But whether losing his mother at such a young age was what convinced him he could live without them, or whether the deciding factor was never knowing who his father was, it's going to take something big to make him finally see that.*

Or maybe not. Faint hope stirred in her. Maybe being back here at the Double B was nurturing the growth of some of those roots. He and Del were still at loggerheads with one another much of the time, but lately a grudging respect took the edge off their disagreements. Every day more of the barriers she sensed in her own relationship with Gabe seemed to fall. And although he still asserted that he had no interest in reclaiming any ties to his Dineh heritage, and only set foot on the Dinetah when he had business there, surely his gift to Emma of the moccasins and Navajo-crafted bracelet showed that he wasn't so estranged from his culture as he liked to think.

*You're clutching at straws,* an annoying voice inside her head informed her. *And deep down, you know it. If you truly believed he'd made peace with his past and himself, by now you'd have told him the truth about Emily, instead of letting him continue to believe Larry fathered—*

"I guess it's useless to deny it." Steve's belligerent tone cut through her thoughts. "Yeah, I was setting up a nice little retirement fund for myself at Jess's expense. I thought I'd be long gone by the time he discovered what I'd done, but them's the breaks. It didn't work out that way."

He stood, ignoring the two men on the other side

of the table from him and fixing a sullen glare on Gabe. "Your bully-boys can escort me to my bank and watch over me while I arrange to have the Milagro Construction amounts transferred back into the Crawford Solutions' general account, but with Jess dead, I don't see why that can't be the end of it. I'll resign, of course—"

"Stop playing games, Dixon." Gabe's tone was disgusted. "You know damn well this can't be the end of it, just like you know we're talking about the Dos Abejas millions, not whatever small-time fiddle you also had going with Milagro Construction. You got it right the first time—denying this is useless, so don't try to tell me that some unknown hacker must have broken past the firewalls and security features that protect any company's banking system, and pinned this theft on you. Caro's explained how when a user accesses this program with his password, all transactions done under that password are attributed to him by name. Take a look at the Dos Abejas transfers and tell me whose name is beside them, dammit."

"The Dos Abejas—" Dixon snatched the printout from Gabe's hand with a scowl.

Watching him, Caro felt the same disgust Gabe had displayed rise in her as the vice president scanned it quickly, flipping through the pages and then turning back to the first one again.

Despite what Gabe had just said to him, he was going to deny the evidence he was holding, she thought angrily. Del's hope to lay Jess to rest in a proper grave could be weeks or months away from reality. If Dixon had decided to go down fighting rather than take responsibility for the fiscal crimes he'd committed, there was no way he would ever admit to any knowledge of Jess's kidnapping and death.

Even as her patience ran out, she saw his shoulders slump. His gaze as he dropped the printout on the table was unreadable.

"I never was the type to go on swinging once the game was over," he said, "and this game looks about as wrapped up as it could be. What are your plans for me now, Riggs?"

"I'm turning you over to the feds," Gabe replied. "Embezzlement's the least of the charges they'll be laying against you. Kidnapping, murder, the attempted murder of Caro two days ago that my men tell me you also denied on the drive here." His tone harshened. "For that one alone I hope you never see the light of day again, Dixon."

Steve nodded. "I knew Jess had given her a password to access the accounts, so I had to eliminate her before she started snooping," he said. "Makes sense, doesn't it?"

"I suppose to a monster like you it does," Caro said, taking a step toward him and aware of Gabe's restraining hand on her arm. "What makes no sense at all is why you threatened the life of my baby."

"What's with the telephone repair vehicle parked out—"

Del's query as he opened the screen door behind Dixon to let Greta enter the kitchen ahead of him was abruptly broken off. Taking in the situation immediately, he reached for Greta as Gabe thrust Caro behind him and made a grab for Dixon.

They were both too late.

In frozen horror Caro saw Steve Dixon viciously yank Greta in front of him and wrest the rifle she was holding from her startled grasp. In a second quick motion he levered the bolt up, snapped back the firing mechanism and brought the bolt down again as he thrust the barrel of the rifle under Greta's chin. He looked around the room with glittering eyes.

"Anyone tries to stop me, the lady gets it first," he snarled as he began backing toward the door.

# Chapter Eleven

"I'll let her go as soon as I make the main road, Riggs," Steve went on. "Phone up to your man on the gate and tell him to let us through."

"I can't do that, Dixon. How do I know you'll keep to—"

"This isn't your call, Gabe," Del said curtly. He inclined his head at Dixon. "Take me as your hostage instead."

"I don't think so." The sound that came from Steve was almost too rusty to be a laugh. "I'm holding the high cards. Why should I give them up?"

"Then, I'll phone through to Joseph Tahe at the guard shack right now," Del said, his even tone belying the fear in his eyes. "And you have my word on it that no one will come after you until you're off the property and my wife's been released."

Watching Del, Caro saw that his keen gaze never left Dixon, but his next words were directed at Greta. "Baby-girl, we'll get you out of this safely. That's a promise."

"I know, you tough old mustang," Greta shakily

replied before her words were cut off by Dixon tightening his arm-hold around her neck.

"Not good enough, Hawkins." He blinked at Del. "That's who you are, right? Jess's famous Lieutenant Hawkins?" At Del's nod he continued. "I'll take the truck I was brought here in, but first I'll see you shoot the phone connection to the house and the tires on the other two vehicles standing in the yard."

"You've got my weapon," Del pointed out steadily. "My wife was carrying it for me because I have trouble making it up the porch steps when I don't have my cane."

Dixon nodded in comprehension. "Jess told me that about you, too, that you'd lost your legs in 'Nam. Take a pistol from one of my former escorts."

"Give Del your gun, Terry," Gabe said, as the taller of the two ex–Recoveries International men hesitated.

Grimacing, the man bent down and removed a deadly looking automatic from a holster concealed under his pant leg, just above his work boot. He handed it to Del.

"Phone the guard at the gate," Dixon reminded Del tersely. He glanced at Gabe. "Lucky for me your boys aren't real linesmen, Riggs. I wouldn't want the next call from the Double B to be to the local sheriff's office, which is why I'm going to have Hawkins take care of that eventuality."

"What if that scumbag decides to hold on to his hostage?"

The low-voiced question came from the man Gabe had called Terry, as Del and Dixon and Greta descended the porch steps and made their way across the yard to the parked vehicles.

"He needs her to get out of here, but after that he'll make more speed alone," Gabe said, watching through the screen door as Del aimed the pistol at the old-style connector at the top of the telephone pole by the drive. "I think Dixon will do exactly what he promised, but in case I'm wrong I'm going to cut across the west corner of the property. If I leave right after he does, I'll get to the main road in time to make sure he lets Greta go unharmed."

Del fired four more shots in fast succession, and Caro saw the farm utility sink down to its rims.

"*How?*" she asked Gabe urgently. "It's not possible—not without transportation of some kind."

"This is a ranch, princess," he said with a humorless smile. "And on a ranch, as long as you've got a horse you've got transportation…even if the only horse in the barn right now is a bad-tempered, hammerheaded Appaloosa."

IT HAD FALLEN TO HER to break the news of the events of this afternoon not once, but three times in the hours that had followed Steve's escape, Caro thought wryly that evening. Daniel and MacLeish had returned from their fencing chore only minutes after Gabe had mounted bareback on a rearing Chorizo and had ridden at top speed across the west quarter of the property, disappearing from sight almost immediately over a small rise in the terrain. Del, looking older than Caro had ever seen him before, had gotten into Daniel's battered pickup, and the three ex-marines had roared out of the yard, only to return a while later with a white-faced and dazed-looking Greta.

Greta hadn't protested when her husband had declared his intention of getting her to a hospital right away.

"Maybe that would be best, sweetie," she'd agreed, pressing a shaking hand to her stomach. "I feel like I've got a bushel basket of butterflies swooping around in here. I'd better get my blood pressure checked."

After their departure Caro had filled in the details for Mac and Daniel, who'd only received a sketchy account from Del. Even as she'd been finishing her recitation and Mac had been heading for one of the equipment sheds with the two former Recoveries International men to get some replacement tires for the crippled vehicles, Connor had returned from his meeting in Albuquerque with the Bureau, and she'd begun her story all over again for his benefit.

Tess and Susannah had been the last to arrive back at the ranch, after a day spent in town taking nine-year-old Joey to the dentist, buying some much-needed outfits for Susannah's rapidly growing baby boy, Danny, and doing the weekly grocery shopping. By then Gabe had returned, too, with a lathered but still feisty Chorizo, but since Caro had no intention of trading places with him and rubbing down the volatile Appaloosa in return for Gabe bringing Tess and Susannah up to speed on what had happened, once more she'd launched into her tale.

The phone connection had been repaired in the past hour, and soon Tye would be calling from Mexico with his daily progress report, she thought now as she began helping Tess and Susannah unpack the groceries. Someone else could fill him in on the situation.

"But Greta's really all right?" Based on the friendship that had formed between them before she'd come to the Double B, Susannah had the closest bond with Greta and her worry showed.

"Just shaken, which is why Del insisted on taking her to Gallup where she can stay overnight for observation in the hospital." Caro smiled in reassurance. "Gabe's fine, too, even though Chorizo got spooked a few times during Gabe's ride to Last Chance to tell Sheriff Bannerman to alert the FBI and put an APB out on Dixon."

"I'll feel better when we hear the police have found Dixon and taken him into custody," Tess said fiercely, stowing several cartons of ice cream into the freezer compartment of the refrigerator and glancing past the screen door to the porch, where Joey was playing with Chorrie, his puppy. "What kind of monster kills a friend for money and then—"

Her angry words were interrupted by the shrilling of the wall-mounted telephone beside her, and she grabbed up the receiver with a worried frown.

"Hello?" Her frown smoothed out. "Oh, hi, Tyler. Let me hand you over to Sus—"

Watching her, Caro saw Tess's eyes close momentarily. When they opened again they were filled with pain.

"I—I see," she said quietly, meeting Caro's gaze. "Yes, I'll tell the others, Tye, but I'm sure you want to tell Susannah yourself. Here she is."

Even as Tess handed the receiver to Susannah, Gabe entered from the porch. He took one look at Tess's drawn features, and his own hardened.

"Bad news?" Mindful of Joey's presence just beyond the screen door, he kept his voice low, as did Tess when she answered him.

"Not bad, just sad." She shook her head unhappily. "Tyler says the *federales* have found a body matching Jess's description. They'll allow him to view it at the morgue sometime tomorrow to make a positive identification."

"DON'T SAY I never take you anywhere, lady."

Behind the wheel of Connor's sedan, Gabe shot Caro, in the passenger seat beside him, a smile that belied the gravelled roughness of his tone. She smiled back at him, quenching the guilty ripple that ran through her as she did.

The events of the previous day—their discovery of Dixon's theft from Crawford Solutions, his confession and escape with Greta as hostage, Tye's news from Mexico—had been so overwhelmingly grim that her current lightheartedness didn't seem entirely appropriate. But appropriate or not, Caro thought helplessly, she *did* feel lighthearted. When Gabe had issued this unexpected invitation to accompany him, she'd had no trouble enlisting Tess and Susannah to baby-sit Emily. Now the prospect of a whole day with Gabe stretched out in front of her, a day free of the fear that had dogged her since Jess's kidnapper had issued his threat against her child. Even the fact that they were on their way to Albuquerque to question

Larry Kanin at the head office of Recoveries International couldn't dim her mood.

"Now, why would I say that?" she replied innocently. "Just because you kept me under what amounted to house arrest on a horse-ranch-slash-teen-boot-camp for two weeks and practically tore a strip off me everytime I set foot outside the door?"

"Point taken." The hard angles of his face broke into another wry grin, and then his expression sobered. "I guess you've had enough of ranch life to last you for quite a while, haven't you. Real ranch life, I mean," he added dryly, "since I don't count the Lazy J with its indoor swimming pool and air-conditioning and home-theater screening room as a real ranch."

"Jess never did, either." It was hard to talk about him, Caro thought wistfully, but it would be harder still to let the good memories fade. She managed a small laugh. "He always said that if he'd wanted real ranch life he'd have signed on as a hand at the Double B. But you know, I don't think the trappings of his success were ever that important to him. I really believe that if he'd lost his fortune, as long as he had enough left to continue working with his beloved computers he would have been perfectly happy. And as for me…no, I haven't had enough of ranch life," she said slowly.

She glanced at him in surprise. "I didn't know I was going to say that," she admitted. "In fact, when we first arrived at the Double B, I remember wondering how Greta and Susannah and Tess could stand living so far away from the amenities. But after a couple of days there I realized that all the amenities I needed were right in front of me.''

''Such as?'' Gabe met her glance.

''Such as good friends, fresh air, beauty everywhere I looked. No, I'm not looking forward to leaving the Double B, Gabe.''

''Good. Because until Dixon's caught and we know for certain who he was working with, I wouldn't recommend it anyway.''

It was a more pragmatic answer than she'd been hoping for from him, she thought. Then again, if and when Gabe ever did talk of a future with her, it wouldn't be while he was exiting a freeway and merging with city traffic. She decided to change the subject.

''I guess Greta must have been more shaken up than I'd realized, to have to stay in the hospital for a few extra days while the doctors run more tests on her. Is Del planning to remain in Gallup while they do?''

''Greta won't let him. She told him he was driving her crazy, fussing around and hovering at her bedside, so she insisted he come home today.'' Gabe signaled a turn and slowed. ''Del didn't say, but I wondered whether the doctors found something unrelated to her ordeal when they checked her over.'' His mouth firmed to a line. ''I hated having to hit him with Tye's news at such a bad time, but I know he wouldn't have thanked me for keeping it from him.''

''How did he react?''

''With grief, mixed with relief over the fact that Jess will finally be able to be brought home and laid to rest.'' He frowned. ''And with some guilt. Apparently his last conversation with Jess ended in an argument, and naturally he wishes now that it hadn't.''

''An argument over what?'' Caro asked in astonishment. ''For heaven's sake, Jess was the easiest-going man I've ever known. And despite Del's crustiness, I always had the impression he and Jess didn't rub each other the wrong way like he and—''

She stopped abruptly. A corner of Gabe's mouth curved up.

''Hell, go ahead and say it, honey. Like Del and me, right? I agree, there was never that kind of friction between them, but from what Del told me, he was forced into taking a hard line with Jess this time.'' He looked uncomfortable. ''Jess came to the Double B a few weeks before his trip to Mexico with some crazy story about Del being his father.''

She'd been astonished a moment ago, Caro thought. Now she was flabbergasted. ''But what would have made him believe such a thing?'' she protested in shock. ''I know from Greta that Del and Jess's mother knew each other way back when, but that's hardly enough to accuse a man of fathering you and then shirking his responsibilities to you.''

''It might be enough if you were Jess and grew up wishing it were true.'' Gabe exhaled loudly. ''He hero-worshiped Del from the start. He saw being sent to the Double B as a dream come true when he was a teen, and at one time or another he floated his theory about Del being his father to all of us—me, Connor and Tye. In our sensitive juvenile-delinquent way we told him he was nuts, of course, but one thing we never knew was that the day before our year was up he actually went to Del and confronted him with his suspicions. I only found that out from Del yesterday.''

''I don't understand. When Jess was a teen he asked Del if he was his father, and although Del set him straight then, he never totally discarded that belief?'' Caro bit her lip. ''Oh, Gabe, how sad that seems.''

''Del saw it as sad, too. But he said he still couldn't let Jess continue thinking something that just wasn't true, especially when Jess admitted that his mother hadn't put the idea into his head.''

''And their meeting probably ended in them both saying things they didn't mean,'' Caro said softly. ''I can understand why Del feels guilty over that, but he's right. What choice did he have but to set Jess straight?'' A thought occurred to her, and her expression brightened. ''Jess must have come to that conclusion himself after he'd thought it over, Gabe. Remember his phone call to Tye—the one where he said he wanted a meeting with all the Double B's when he got back from Mexico?''

''The one where he said he'd found a link between everything that had happened recently at the ranch, and Del's past in Vietnam?'' A slow grin broke across Gabe's features. ''I think you've got something, princess. He'd hardly have wanted to run his latest theory by Del for his approval if he hadn't finally given up on the old one. I'll remind Del of that. It might relieve him of some of that guilt he's feeling.''

He pulled into a parking space and switched off the engine before turning to her. ''We're not out of the woods yet with this investigation, although Connor's meeting with his FBI contact today to discuss their progress in the search for Andrew Scott is a good sign. Connor hopes it means that yesterday's events have convinced the Bureau to throw all their resources at bringing him in and questioning him about his connection to Dixon. Even if they don't locate Scott immediately, Dixon himself can't run for long—especially since the authorities have frozen his bank accounts and flagged his passport at every border crossing. So soon he'll be in custody, and at that point you and Emily will be free to go back to the Lazy J while Jess's estate is being settled, or find your own place here in Albuquerque if you'd prefer.''

"Not here." She had no idea where this conversation was going, Caro thought, puzzled. "In Albuquerque I'm William Moore's daughter, Gabe. I've come to appreciate being my own woman, and whether or not my father ever tries to mend the breach between us and have a relationship with his granddaughter, I don't see myself ever slipping back into my old life again.''

"Somehow I don't see that, either, princess." His tone was wry. He reached across the space between them and lightly tucked a short strand of her hair behind her ear, letting his hand rest there as he continued. "And I don't see myself slipping back into the desert. The day after I resigned from Recoveries International I got phone calls from three other hostage negotiation firms, all offering me a job. I'm going back into the field when this is over, Caro.''

The amber gaze watching her deepened to near-black. "In my line of work I'm usually out of the country, but I get back here for flying visits several times a year. I'd like to be able to come and see you and Emily when I do."

The street they were parked on was filled with traffic. On the sidewalk passersbys went about their business. After her time at the Double B, Caro thought disjointedly, she found the constant background noise of a city almost overwhelming.

Which made it all the more amazing that she'd just heard the tiny *crack* of her own heart breaking.

She'd been a fool. The man had told her from the start that he was a loner, but still she'd allowed herself to daydream about Emily having a full-time daddy, about herself having the kind of future with Gabe that Susannah and Tess had won with their Double B ex— bad boys.

*You allowed yourself to daydream, yes. But be honest—did you ever believe those daydreams would come true?*

"Not really," she said softly, meeting the gaze of the man she loved. "That's why I never told you about—"

"Sorry, princess?" A faint frown drew his eyebrows together. "Was that a no or a yes?"

Caro blinked, and with the slightest of movements drew away from him enough so that his hand fell from her hair. The smile she produced felt too bright, but it was the best she could do.

"That's an 'I need time to think about it,' Gabe," she said lightly. "And as you say, we still have a little time before we're in a position to make decisions about what will happen when this is all behind us, right?''

"Right." His smile was apologetic. "Bad timing on my part, especially with this meeting with Larry ahead of us.''

This was a topic she could deal with, Caro thought numbly. She needed to seize it before Gabe started talking about them again.

"You know he's going to deny Steve ever hinted to him that it might not be such a tragedy if Jess didn't come out of that negotiation alive," she said briskly as they exited the sedan. "Even though we don't really believe that his actions during that handover were anything more than a bid for glory that backfired terribly on Larry, just admitting to discussing the death of the hostage he was supposed to keep safe would veer dangerously close to conspiracy to commit murder.''

"I expect him to deny it," Gabe said briefly. He held open the glass and stainless steel door of the starkly modern office building that housed the head office of Recoveries International, as Caro preceded him into the lobby. A bank of elevators stood against one granite wall. "But how he denies it is going to tell me whether my suspicions are correct or not. If they are, the FBI can question him further.''

He fell silent for a moment as an elevator arrived and a woman with a briefcase got out, but as they entered the car and the doors closed behind him he went on, his tone brittle.

"This one was personal, Caro, and I intend to gather every damning scrap of evidence I can against

Dixon. I won't risk him beating these charges because I didn't go the extra mile to put him away.''

He wasn't the same man who'd once sworn to her that he had no ties to the Double B and the friends he had known there, Caro reflected. Gabe had come a long way in the past eight days, and the distance he'd traveled had nothing to do with the number of miles between his desert isolation and a place he'd once thought of as home.

He'd come this far, but no further, she thought achingly. Probably she would never know all the reasons for those few final barriers he kept between himself and the rest of the world—between himself and *her,* she revised. But she couldn't help wondering if the answer to his ultimate alienation might be found on the Dinetah, if he ever allowed himself to go looking for it there.

''What the—''

As the elevator doors opened, Gabe's uncompleted exclamation broke into her thoughts. Immediately she saw what had prompted it.

The wide hallway was a hive of activity, with burly men in movers' uniforms lugging furniture and computers and electronics equipment into an open freight elevator. Even as she looked around her in confusion, Caro heard Larry's angry shout coming from the direction of the office that was being emptied.

''Not that, damn you! That painting's my personal property!''

''We've got our orders, Mr. Kanin.'' One of the muscle-bound men came out of the office with a flat bubble-wrapped package. ''Take it up with the management of this building. All I've been told is that you're three months in arrears on your rent, and they're trying to recoup a fraction of what you owe them.''

''For God's sake, man—'' Larry appeared in the doorway, his face distorted with rage. His gaze landed on Caro and Gabe and his mouth curled into a sneer.

''Great. Just freakin' great. The two people in the world I most want to see at this moment—my ice-queen ex-fiancée who never unfroze enough to give herself to me, and the burned-out case she chose to father her illegitimate brat. Thanks for blowing the whistle on me in Mexico with your buddy Estavez, Riggs. The word got out, and what corporate clients I had left deserted me like rats leaving a—''

His sentence ended abruptly as Gabe's fist crashed into his jaw.

## Chapter Twelve

He had a daughter.

And his child's mother had never intended to tell him he was a father.

Gabe slammed the flat of his hand against the nearest porch pillar, as hard as he could. Even as he stood there, his head bowed and his arm still braced against the pillar, a voice came out of the midnight stillness from a few feet away.

"So she told you, did she?"

The crisp tones were unmistakably Del's—not surprising, since it was his night for guard duty, Gabe belatedly recalled. Del was the last person he wanted to talk to right now. Or no, he corrected himself savagely as he turned away, Caro was the last person, but Del came in a pretty close second.

He couldn't remember much about what had happened at Kanin's office this morning. He remembered hitting him, and he remembered why he'd hit him. It hadn't been because of the bombshell Kanin had dropped on him, since his mind had still been processing what he'd just heard when his fist had decided to get up close and personal with Larry's jaw. It had been because of how he'd referred to Emily.

Caro had once called her baby daughter—*my baby daughter,* Gabe thought, feeling the knife that had been twisting in his gut give another turn—''pure innocence.'' She hadn't lied about that, at least. Emily *was* pure innocence, and from the moment he'd laid eyes on her he'd had the foolish feeling that there was some kind of bond between them. The way she'd clamped onto his finger that first time, the way she held out her arms to him when he bent over her crib, the way she crowed with delight every time he swung her into his arms...

Except that feeling of being bonded with Emily hadn't been foolish. It had been nothing less than the truth. And now that he knew it he wondered why he hadn't been sure of it before.

*Because the snow princess made damn sure you wouldn't see it. And you were so busy looking at those lush lips of hers while she was lying to you that you would have believed her if she'd said black was white, dammit.*

Aside from not remembering much about what had happened in Kanin's office, he also didn't remember most of the drive back to the Double B. He had the feeling she'd tried to talk to him a few times. He was pretty sure he'd seen tears falling from those alpine-blue eyes. In the end she'd fallen silent and had only resumed talking when they were almost at the ranch.

That part he remembered.

''Maybe I should have told you.'' The tears had disappeared from her voice. ''Then when you paid us those flying visits once or twice a year that you were talking about earlier, Emily could have known it was her daddy who was dropping by to say hi.''

It was the first thing she'd said that he'd felt a need to reply to. ''If I'd known I had a child, I wouldn't have—''

''Wouldn't have what? Wouldn't have walked away from us when this investigation was over, wouldn't have contemplated taking the type of job that gives you the perfect excuse not to commit yourself to me, wouldn't have reverted to being a damn loner, Gabe?'' Her voice had shook. ''Oh, I believe you. You would have changed your life out of a sense of duty to the child you created. But I wanted you to do it because you couldn't imagine living without Emily—and without *me*.''

A wave of pain had seemed to rush from her on her last few words, and his immediate response had been anger. What right did the snow princess have to feel pain, when she was the one who'd lied? What right did she have to cry, just because her deception had been found out, and what right did she have to make him feel, even for a moment, that he was in the wrong?

He'd opened his mouth to say all those things, but then the gates of the Double B had come into view. Only when he was pulling into a parking spot by the barn did he speak.

''You don't want me to be part of her life, and I don't want my daughter's world torn apart by one custody dispute after another between her parents. So up to a point I'll bow out. But I won't let you stop me from paying support, and when the time is right, I want her to know who her father is and have the choice of getting to know me. Those terms aren't negotiable.

"And one other thing. I took on the responsibility of keeping you safe. Just because our personal relationship went to hell this afternoon doesn't mean our working one's changed. With any luck, when we walk in, Del or Con will tell us that Steve was picked up by the police while we were gone, Andrew Scott's been found and has confessed to being Dixon's mouthpiece, Leo, and all danger to you and Emily is past. If that's not the case, I think it would be easier for both of us if the whole damn Double B gang doesn't figure out that we're no longer an item."

"So you're changing your rule. The one about nobody gets to pretend." She'd been staring straight at him, so it had been impossible to look away. "Now we pretend, Gabe?"

He'd taken refuge in curtness and had seen the pain that flashed behind her eyes as he did. "Yeah, princess, now we pretend. But you're good at pretense and deception, so it shouldn't be a problem for you."

That last had been a low blow, Gabe thought now, heading for the porch steps. And it hadn't been necessary to say anything about not letting the others know what had happened between them, because when they'd walked into the kitchen together the place had been in an uproar, with Connor's voice raised above everyone else's.

"I know what Tye said Jess told him in that last phone call, dammit! And it's Tye's prerogative to believe that maybe this time one of Jess's half-cocked enthusiasms might have proved to be right and he'd found evidence linking the problems at the Double B to Del's Vietnam past. But although I loved the guy as much as anyone else here, that doesn't stop me from remembering some of Jess's other zany obsessions, and I don't buy into this one, either. Yeah, we were wrong about Andrew Scott, and yeah, now we need to start from scratch to figure out who Leo was, but—"

"We were wrong about Scott? Who says so?" His questions had come out of him in the same parade-ground bark as Del's, Gabe remembered with a touch of embarrassment. But it had served to silence the chatter. Connor had raked a hand through his hair.

"The Bureau says so." His tone had been bitter. "They might have said so days ago, except the officious pencil-pusher who was Scott's FBI contact was more concerned about keeping the juiciest whistle-blowing file he'd ever stumbled across to himself than cooperating with his peers."

He'd nodded grimly at Gabe. "It's true. Scott contacted the feds when he quit Crawford Solutions. Said he'd discovered evidence of financial chicanery on Dixon's part, but when he tried to tell Jess of his findings, Jess refused to hear a word against the man who'd been with him from the start. They almost came to blows over it, and the only reason Scott didn't just keep quiet after that and let Jess go down the tubes was that when he thought it over, he realized he would be doing his country a disservice by allowing Dixon to destroy the company. The Pentagon's only one branch of the government that Jess developed cutting-edge software for,'' he ended heavily.

''So all the time we've been begging the feds to find Scott and bring him in, they've had him tucked away in a safe house somewhere while they've been building a case against Dixon?''

Out of habit, Gabe recalled, he'd looked at Caro as he'd posed his question—to get her reaction. She'd looked back at him with no expression at all in those blue eyes, and for a moment he felt as if he'd just stepped into an elevator and found it wasn't there.

Which was stupid, he thought bitterly.

''That's what Higgins, the pencil-pusher, was so reluctant to divulge,'' Connor had drawled. ''His star witness up and disappeared on him before he could arrange to get him under wraps. My contact at the Bureau says the unofficial take on the situation is that Higgins mishandled Scott so badly that Scott lost confidence in his ability to keep him safe if he testified against Dixon, and decided to give the whole thing up and disappear. But the bottom line still remains, Gabe—Scott isn't Leo. He was gunning for Dixon, not allied with him.''

Maybe that was Connor's bottom line, Gabe thought now as he began to descend the porch steps. It probably should be his, too, but it wasn't.

His bottom line was that Caro had lied to him.

From the darkness came the *thump* of a porch chair's front legs making contact with the floor. ''I figured she must have told you, from the way the two of you looked when you came back from Albuquerque this afternoon. Or maybe...'' Del gave a low whistle. "Yeah, that's how it happened, didn't it. She didn't tell you, but somehow Kanin had figured out who Emmie's daddy was and he spilled the beans."

Gabe whirled around, raw fury spilling through him. He re-mounted the steps two at a time.

"So help me, Hawkins, I've had to take you riding me about everything under the sun since the day I came here, fifteen years ago. But this is off limits, do you hear? *She's* off limits! And if you say one more word on the subject I'll—"

"You'll what, Riggs?" There was a cold edge of contempt in Del's tone. "You'll walk out? Hell, go ahead. That's what she was afraid you'd do, so why not prove her right?"

"You've got it wrong," Gabe said thickly. "She was afraid I'd stay."

A thought struck him, and he stiffened. "You knew, obviously. You knew Emily was my daughter and you kept it from me. There never was that much between us, Hawkins, but what little there was ends here. I'm through with you and the Double B."

"Going back to the desert, Riggs?" Del's voice sharpened. "Or back to the job? It suited you, I'll admit. You got flown into some godforsaken spot, laid your life on the line to bring a father or a son or a mother back to their family, and then you did it all over somewhere else. You put families together again. You made them whole. You were so busy doing that, you never had to think about the gaps in your own life."

"The gaps like having a father who didn't stick around?" Gabe laughed incredulously. "Hell, that was Jess's problem, not mine. I got along all right without an old man, just like Tye did with an absentee father he barely knew and just like Connor, who saw his die when he was a kid. I was a Double B bad boy, Del. Most of us came from backgrounds like that."

"But no one else who came here built such high walls around himself in consequence," Del answered flatly. "And you never really let the barriers down, did you. Not between you and me, not between you and your friends here, not between you and Caro. I went to bat for you when I learned Emily was yours, you know. I tried to convince Caro she should tell you. But she was right not to, I see that now."

There was just enough light for Gabe to see Del's hawklike gaze narrow at him.

"Your little girl's part Dineh, like you. If you never make peace with that part of your heritage, how will you ever pass it on to her when the time comes?" Del's voice lost its edge. "Yeah, whoever your father was, he walked away from you, and I know it must have felt like your mother did, too, when she died. I suspect that's why you decided at an early age to walk out on people yourself, before they could do it to you. But it's time to forgive that Dineh woman who gave birth to you and loved you. It's time to take back the part of you that's her."

Del stood. "I know Alice Tahe's sent messages through Joseph, asking you to come and see her. I know you've ignored those messages. Maybe if you hadn't, you wouldn't have screwed everything up so badly."

Without another word he went into the house. Through the screen door, Gabe saw him set the coffeepot on the stove.

The Lieutenant had lost it, he thought grimly a few minutes later as he strode through the dark yard to the darker silhouette of the horse barn. Maybe it was his worry over Greta that had muddied his thinking, maybe it was the stress of the incidents that had occurred at the Double B over the past few months, but whatever it was, Hawkins had it all wrong.

''Yah-ta-hey, Runner-with-the-Wind.''

He kept his voice low as he approached the stall, but even so, he knew the Appaloosa had heard the traditional Dineh greeting. For the first time in hours he felt a little of the tension drain from him.

Everyone else called the stallion Chorizo. A sixteen-year-old Gabe had taken one look at him and known immediately that that wasn't his real name. He'd privately christened him Runner-with-the-Wind, and although Chorizo had never allowed anyone else to ride him, Runner-with-the-Wind had flown through more than one long-ago dawn with Gabe on his back.

Gabe hesitated, and then unlatched the stall door.

''The moon is a sliver, Runner-with-the-Wind,'' he said softly. He slid one hand into the coarse mane and with the other touched the ruined right side of the stallion's face. Like everyone else at the Double B, he knew the story of how Del had rescued Chorizo as a colt from a brutal owner, but too late to prevent the man from permanently scarring the animal's face and psyche. Unlike almost everyone else, Gabe had never feared that the Appaloosa's famously wicked temper would be turned on him.

"The moon is a sliver, the world is dark, and somewhere on the Dinetah is an old lady. She's probably asleep. If she is, at least we'll have ridden through the night together, and that will be a memory worth making. Shall we go, Runner-with-the-Wind?"

The Appaloosa whickered softly as he was led from the stall. Reaching the open doors of the barn and tightening his grasp on the animal's mane, Gabe swung himself up with unconscious ease.

A stray shaft of starlight cut through the darkness and glimmered faintly on the silver and turquoise cuff banding his left wrist. Gabe frowned, and for no reason at all fear flickered momentarily through him. The horse beneath him whickered again, this time more insistently.

The fear fell away. He took a deep breath. Then he touched his heels to the Appaloosa's flanks, and Runner-with-the-Wind lived up to his Navajo name.

Forever after, Gabriel Riggs never forgot that ride through the dark to the Dinetah. Neither, he suspected, did the horse everyone else called Chorizo. At some point they seemed no longer to be two separate beings, but to have melded into a single, perfectly balanced entity.

And at some point Gabe became dimly aware that he wasn't riding alone.

That part he never recalled very clearly. When he tried to afterward, he found he could only bring to mind impressions—impressions of others keeping pace with him in the night; impressions of triumphant cries echoing all around him—cries in a language that weren't English, but that he found he could understand easily; impressions of copper-tan skin like his, straight dark hair like his, brief flashes of white as his shadowy companions smiled at him in recognition and welcome.

And then they were gone—if, as he wondered for the rest of his life, they had ever really been there and hadn't been phantasms conjured up by the exhilaration he'd felt during his ride. They were gone, he was on the Dinetah, and although he had never visited Alice Tahe before, Gabe knew with certainty that the traditional hivelike structure he was looking at was her hogan.

He slipped from the Appaloosa's back, and with that same unsettling certainty knew there was no need to secure the animal.

"You are late, my son."

For a man who'd always figured he had steady nerves, Gabe came pretty damn close to jumping about a foot in the air. He could barely make out the small, sturdy figure of the old lady standing by the entrance to her hogan.

"Late, Grandmother?" It seemed right to address her that way. "I came as fast as I could."

The dreamlike state he'd been in during that wild ride through the dark suddenly dissipated, and cold sanity returned. *Okay, Hawkins,* Gabe thought, *I came to the Dinetah. I saw Alice Tahe, like you said. And now I think I'll just turn around and go—*

"You *delayed* as long as you could." There was sharp condemnation in the old lady's voice. "Even now, when there may be no time left, you delay. But you are the only one of the three who ever came at all, my son, and that may yet save those he wishes to destroy. Come, all is ready.''

Without waiting for his reply, Alice Tahe turned and entered her hogan. And after a moment's hesitation, Gabe followed.

The first thing he noticed was the dry, spicy scent of some kind of grass being burned. A thin tendril of smoke rose from a scraped-out hollow in the center of the neatly brushed earth floor of the hogan, and he realized that the spicy scent was coming from the smudge-fire smoldering there. The smell wasn't unpleasant—the opposite, in fact—but the smoke drifting through the room stung his eyes enough to make them water a little.

Alice Tahe's eyes, however, were bright and snapping in their nests of wrinkles. Del had said she'd seen her hundredth birthday, and looking at her, Gabe believed it. She wore the traditional dress of a Dineh woman, a many-tiered skirt topped by a silver-buttoned, velveteen blouse, and her hair was pulled into a tight bun at the back of her head and bound by white yarn, also in the traditional Navajo way.

He felt suddenly ashamed of the churlish way he'd put off coming to see her, and of his impatience a moment ago. She'd gone to some trouble to set the stage for what she wanted to say to him, obviously, although how she'd known he would come tonight he still hadn't figured out. But that didn't matter right now. What mattered was that an old lady who still clung to the ancient beliefs and stories of her ancestors had welcomed him into her home. The least he could do in return for her courtesy was to listen with respect to her, agree with whatever she had to say, and then take his leave of her, again with the respect her age deserved.

"You think that is how this meeting will go, my son?" Those snapping eyes lit briefly with a flash of humor as they looked at him. "Humoring an old lady, leaving with a polite smile? I had heard you had strayed far from the path. I didn't know how far. Sit."

How the *hell* had she read his mind like that? Gabe realized his mouth was open and closed it hastily.

"I said sit! Your time is running out!"

Below the quick anger in her tone was a more elusive emotion. As he followed her example and lowered himself to a cross-legged position on the opposite side of the smudge-fire from her, he realized what that emotion was.

Fear.

Alice Tahe was desperately afraid. It was there in her voice, it was in the slight trembling of her hands that he'd taken for an effect of her advanced years, it was all around him in the close, smoky atmosphere of her hogan. She was terrified. And her terror had a name.

*"Skinwalker…"*

The voice inside his head sounded exactly like Alice Tahe's. Gabe realized that his eyes had fallen closed, most likely to shut out the smoke, and he snapped them open again.

She was asleep. Her head had sunk down onto her chest and her breathing was deep and sonorous. A

smile touched the corners of his lips. Feisty as she
was, when you came down to it, she was just an old
lady who'd stayed up half the night waiting for him,
and she'd fallen—

*SILENCE!*

This time Gabe did jump. His startled gaze took in
Alice's still-bowed head, her closed eyes, her closed
and wrinkled lips. It had been her voice he'd heard.
But that was...impossible.

*Impossible in the Belacana world. Not in the Dineh
one. You are lucky—you can cross back and forth
between the two, although until now you have not
chosen to do so. You have lost your way, haven't you,
my son.*

There was compassion now in that unspoken voice.
But he didn't need compassion from a woman he
didn't know, Gabe thought uncomfortably, especially
since there was no reason for an old Dineh lady to
feel sorry for him.

He opened his mouth to tell her so as politely as
possible, but before he could, he heard a second voice
in his head.

*Yes, Grandmother, I have. I lost it so long ago that
I don't even know when I took the wrong path. And
only recently have I realized I'm the only one trav-
eling this lonely road, and that if I keep on it I'll lose
my soul.*

The second voice was his own. But he hadn't spoken those words, Gabe thought in confusion. He
hadn't even *intended* to say them. They'd just come
out of...

...his innermost thoughts. Even as the incredible

realization hit him, Alice Tahe spoke—except that wasn't what she was doing at all, any more than he had been.

*You are right. Your soul is in jeopardy. But until a man knows where to find his soul, how can he keep it safe? That is the first question I ask you, and one you must answer for yourself. My second question is no question, but a warning—there is an evil that walks like a man and talks like a man. But this evil is no man, it is a ghost.*

*The ghost our people call Skinwalker.* His eyes closed, Gabe nodded. *The Dineh legends say he can take whatever form he wishes and—*

*Skinwalker is no legend!* The sharpness had returned to her. *He is real and he means to bring death to all you hold dear. Coming here has given you strength, but you need to be stronger still. And there is no more time....*

"The past has become the present. The circle has come around."

With a small shock Gabe realized that Alice Tahe had spoken the last two sentences aloud. He opened his eyes, and through the now-swirling smoke he saw her gaze fix on him.

"The past has become the present and the circle has come around? I don't understand," he began, but she cut him off.

"You must find understanding. Your child's life depends on it—her life, and the life of her mother. Now go. Take my prayers with you, my son, and *go!*"

The smudge-fire flared suddenly up and the smoke

billowed thickly. Gabe tried to get to his feet but the choking miasma overwhelmed him. He made a second attempt, and this time he seemed to feel strong arms helping him up and bearing him out of the hogan.

"The past has become the present. The circle has come around. The past has become the present. The circle has..." Still muttering Alice's cryptic phrase, groggily he raised his head. Somehow he had ended up back on his hands and knees again, he thought in frustration. He reached blindly out in front of him, and felt something. He grasped it and hauled himself to his feet.

"Stay where you are, mister! I've got a double-barreled shotgun pointed right at you."

The unmistakable sound of a bolt-action being levered into place accompanied the crisp warning. A moment later light flooded the scene, and instinctively Gabe threw up an arm to shield his eyes.

But not before he saw who had delivered the warning. It was Del, and he was standing only feet away...

...on the porch of the Double B.

## Chapter Thirteen

"Let's see if I've got this right. One second you were at Alice Tahe's hogan, and the next thing you knew you were here at the Double B looking down the barrel of my gun?" Del's grunt was disgusted. "Hell, when I checked the barn a few minutes ago at your request to make sure Chorizo was back in his stall, maybe I should have looked for an empty bottle or two. I've never known you to handle your problems by drowning them in alcohol before, Riggs, but I guess there's a first time for everything. Go sleep it off, and let everyone else get back to their beds, too."

A spark of anger flared in Caro. Crustiness was one thing, but as was all too usual when he was confronting Gabe, Del had just stepped over the line. About to tell him so, she suddenly stopped herself.

Gabriel Riggs didn't need her to go to bat for him. Gabriel Riggs had made it clear that he didn't need Caro Moore, period. And although for a while she'd begun to hope that situation might have changed, today she'd realized that it never would.

His idea of a future with her had been to remove himself as far as possible from her presence—to go back to a job that, from his description of his previous employment, would have him in Italy one week and an obscure South American state the next, with scarcely any downtime in between.

*Of course, that was before he knew I'd kept the truth about his daughter from him,* she reminded herself unhappily. *Now he not only doesn't want a future with me, he's made it plain he regrets our past—all except for one part of it.*

That part was Emily. He'd adored her even before he'd known she was his. And that was why Del's accusation was not only over the line, Caro thought slowly, but totally unjustified.

Yes, Gabe's story was unbelievable. At his insistence, everyone except Susannah and Tess, who were with their own children at Tess's house, had assembled in the kitchen of the Double B to hear it, and Caro suspected her own face had shown the same baffled incredulity as Con's and Daniel's and John MacLeish's at Gabe's recounting of his eerily unsettling encounter with Alice Tahe. But the clincher for them all had been his reluctant admission to Del that he had no idea how he'd made his way back to the ranch, and no memory of having done so.

So his story was unbelievable…but the urgency with which he'd told it rang true. And while he was responsible for keeping his little daughter safe, Caro thought, the last thing Emily's father would do was get drunk.

''I guess I can't blame you for jumping to that conclusion, Hawkins.'' It was obvious from Gabe's controlled tone that he was keeping his temper with difficulty. "I know parts of this sound crazy—"

"Try *all* of it," Del interjected.

"—but however she got her information, I think Alice stumbled on the truth," Gabe continued, ignoring Del. He took a deep breath. "The past has become the present. The circle has come around. There's only one thing that could mean."

"You're talkin' about the Beta Beta link," Daniel Bird, Susannah's father and Del's old comrade, said softly. He looked down at his hands. "I always suspicioned it would turn out to be connected to what's been happenin' at the ranch. Somethin' inside me knew the past wasn't done with us yet."

"Well, I'm done with the past," Del said sharply. He favored Gabe with an icy stare. "Yesterday my wife was abducted by that son of a bitch Dixon. She's still in the hospital getting over the trauma. I don't give a pinch of horsesh—" he shot a glance at Caro "—a damn about this new theory of yours, Riggs. Dixon was behind Jess's kidnapping and death, and he all but came straight out and confessed he'd targeted Caro and Emily because the password Jess had provided Caro with when he gave her access to his business affairs meant she could do exactly what she did—search Crawford Solutions' bank records and discover the phony Dos Abejas payoffs. Besides, only a guilty man would have bolted like he did when he saw the evidence we had on him."

His tone was hostile, and Caro stared at him. This was a side of Del she hadn't seen before, she thought in dismay. Whereas his previous altercations with

Gabe had been more in the nature of two strong-minded men disagreeing with each other, this time he—

Del turned stiffly away and lifted the coffeepot from the stove. As he did, she saw the tremor, instantly stilled, that shook his hand.

Ex-Marine Lieutenant Hawkins was afraid. Even as the impossible thought came to her, Caro knew she was right. He'd tried to hide it with a show of aggression, but he was afraid.

"There's no harm in letting Riggs tell us what his theory is, old buddy." John MacLeish sounded puzzled. "After all, we can't say we have the case all wrapped up just yet, not when we don't know who Leo is."

"That's not really true, Mac." Caro realized that in her agitation she'd spoken too loudly. She went on more quietly. "I think Del *does* know who Leo is— or at least, he's afraid he does. Am I right, Del?"

"I don't know what you're—"

She cut across his frosty rejoinder. "You could handle it when it was Jess's theory. You could even handle it when I wondered if the logo on the side of the kidnappers' truck meant we should look into your Vietnam past. But all Gabe would concede to was that someone might be using the Beta Beta Force connection as a smoke screen, so you allowed yourself to dismiss it, too."

She turned to Gabe, and even at such a moment she found her gaze lingering on the hard planes of his face as if she were imprinting them on her memory. "He always rode you hardest for a reason," she said unevenly. "He saw in you the man you could be, Gabe—and he knew that man would be someone he could respect. Tonight you became that man when you went to see Alice Tahe on the Dinetah and made peace with a part of yourself you've denied for too long. But you also came back convinced that the Beta Beta connection's real, and although Del's managed to dismiss that theory from everyone else, he can't when it comes from you."

She waited for Gabe's response. When it came it wasn't what she'd expected.

"You did the right thing, princess," he said slowly. "You wanted our daughter to have a full-time father, not a stranger who showed up every once in a while and then broke her heart by leaving again. The Gabe Riggs I was this afternoon didn't get that. The man who came back from the Dinetah tonight does."

He held her gaze a moment longer, then he turned to Del. "I need to hear it from you, Hawkins. Do you really think I've gone over the edge with this Beta Beta theory, or is it like Caro says—you're so afraid it could be true that you'd rather close your eyes to it than let this investigation go any further?"

"I think you've gone over the—" Del's crisp tone faltered. His hawklike gaze slid away from Gabe's and then went to each of the others at the table in turn, ending with Caro. A corner of his mouth lifted wryly. "Too damn pretty and too damn smart, aren't you, darlin'?" he growled. "Just like my Greta."

His sigh was heavy. "I'm afraid it could be true, Riggs. I think Leo could fit our first profile—a Vietnam vet who's harbored a hatred against the Double B's all these years for the death of a friend at the hands of Zeke Harmon. And it's not just the two bees symbolism that's convinced me, it's the loose ends we never tied up from the other two cases that have happened here over the past few months—the killer who targeted Susannah, and the people who were after Tess. Except, there's one big difference between those cases and this one.''

''The difference being that targeting Susannah was a way of getting back at her father, Daniel,'' Connor said with a frown. ''And the killers who tried to eliminate Tess and Joey were really after MacLeish. If this mysterious Leo's method of operation is to ally himself with people who have their own unrelated agendas, like that killer Scudder had with Susannah, for example, why did he choose to work with Dixon?'' He shook his head. ''Jess was one of the ranch's bad boys a long time ago and he'd kept in touch with Del, but again, there wasn't the same kind of close relationship between them that there was between Daniel and Suze—a father and a—''

''A father and a daughter?'' Gabe said thinly. ''No. But according to Jess there was a father-son relationship between him and Del. I think his stubborn belief in that caused his death.''

Del had looked shaken before, but now there was a haggardness to his features. ''Leo's plan was to punish me for whatever loss he suffered at the hands of a renegade Beta Beta Force member by killing a man he thought was my son?''

''Your son, the woman your son was going to

marry, and the child he would have raised as his own.''

Caro saw the flash of anguish that came and went behind Gabe's eyes as he answered Del, and knew with a pang that she was responsible for putting it there. A moment ago he had said she'd been right in keeping the truth about Emily from him. She'd told herself the same thing, and had believed it. But at the sight of his pain when he contemplated how close he'd come to never knowing he'd fathered a daughter, for the first time she felt an unsettling doubt as to whether any justification was enough to excuse what she'd done.

*Did I really have a right to decide that he wouldn't be an acceptable father for Emily?* she asked herself. *When I got pregnant with her, I certainly wasn't mother material. How would I have felt if someone had taken her away from me?*

He was still talking. With difficulty she attempted to focus on what he was saying.

''Leo's scheme dovetailed perfectly with Dixon's. I just haven't figured out how he found out what Steve was planning, in order to put himself in a position where Steve would give him a part to play.''

''It doesn't wash, Riggs,'' Del said suddenly. The haggard look left his face and relief took its place. ''Jess was a year older than Con and Gabe. I would have been serving out my last year in 'Nam when he was conceived, so if this Leo did even the most rudimentary checking of the dates, he would have—''

''San Francisco, Lieutenant,'' Daniel said in his soft drawl. He looked up from his hands. ''Three days

R and R. It was just before everything started to go bad that last year, and all of us Double B's were given leave together. That shy little girl from your hometown came all the way out to the coast to see you, and you took her and us out to dinner one night. We had ourselves a right fine time, too, if I remember rightly.''

''I don't think I like what you're implying, Daniel.'' Del's words were clipped. ''I saw Sheila Crawford as a sister, damn you, and if you think I took advantage of her—''

''If you'd stop pulling rank on everyone here and listen for one second, Hawkins, maybe we could get somewhere,'' Gabe broke in. ''Daniel's just saying it's not impossible Jess could have been your son.'' He grimaced. ''Oh, hell. What I mean to say is, it's not impossible that Leo might *think*—''

''I get what Daniel means. I get what you mean, too.'' His fists clenched, Del took a step toward Gabe. ''You think Jess might not have been so off base about who his father was as I always said he was, dammit. Do you want to back up what you just said by accepting the invitation I extended to you the night you arrived, Riggs?''

''If I thought I could knock some sense into that hard head of yours, yeah!'' Gabe exploded. He thrust his face close to Del's. ''But that won't happen, will it, Lieutenant. You're so used to giving orders and keeping everyone else in line that it doesn't ever occur to you that *you* might get it wrong sometimes.''

''It doesn't occur to me that *I* might get it wrong?'' Del gave a bark of laughter. ''That's pretty good, coming from you. Hell, even when you were a teen you thought you knew it all, Riggs, and you haven't changed a—''

*''Stop it, both of you!''*

Caro was on her feet before she was aware of what she was doing. She looked from Gabe's angry face to Del's furious one, took in their identically rigid jaws and tight expressions, and braced herself against the table to keep from swaying.

*The past has become the present. The circle has come around...* As the words resounded in her mind, for an instant the atmosphere in the Double B kitchen seemed filled with the scent of something smoldering, like the smoke from a grass fire. She shook her head to clear it.

''It *couldn't* be true,'' she breathed, her gaze frozen on the scowling men in front of her. ''But it has to be. You two couldn't be anything but—''

''Anything but what, dammit?'' both Gabe and Del growled simultaneously as she paused.

She chose her words carefully. ''Del, you once told me you had a rehab nurse the year after you came back from Vietnam. I...I got the impression she was someone very special to you. What was her name?''

The ex-marine blinked. ''What's that got to do with—'' Something in her expression seemed to alert him, and his frown faded. ''Mary Morgan,'' he said quietly. ''That was her married name. Her husband Robert was listed as 'missing in action' only weeks after their wedding, but she never gave up hope that he would come back to her. Not until the day she got a telegram notifying her that his body had finally been found, that is. What are you getting at, Caro?''

She ignored him and turned to Gabe. He knew, she thought as she saw the stunned disbelief in his eyes. He knew what she was about to say, even if he couldn't accept it yet.

''I remember you saying that when you ended up in the foster system, Gabe, you only had two things to remind you of who you were and where you came from. You've held on to them all these years. One of them is a watch-brooch—a watch-brooch that hangs upside down, like a nurse would wear pinned to her uniform. The other's on your wrist right now.''

''Yeah, and there's a name stamped inside this cuff, princess,'' Gabe said tightly. ''It says *H. Morgan.* I also remember telling you that Harry Morgan's one of the most famous Navajo silversmiths, and like all of the good ones, he has his name stamped on the inside of every piece he makes, to identify himself as the artisan.''

''But this piece has the top of the *H* deliberately scored across by the man who once owned it, to make it into an *R,* Gabe,'' she said softly ''As in Robert Morgan, the husband who never came home to Del's rehab nurse, Mary…and who left his widow only memories…and the silver and turquoise bracelet her son wears today.''

She shook her head, still holding his gaze. ''The real proof of who your father is isn't either of those things, though. It's been staring both of you in the face ever since you arrived back here, no longer a teen but a grown man. Your mom might have reverted back to her maiden name of Riggs when she knew her husband was dead and the child she was bearing had been fathered by a man who was still trying to put the pieces of his life back together, a man she must have decided was still too shattered to cope with the responsibilities of being a father. But when Del knew her, her name was Mary Morgan. All anyone has to do is look at the two of you right now to see you're his son.''

''She's right.'' Connor was looking at Del and Gabe as if he'd never seen them before—or at least, Caro thought, as if he'd never seen what was suddenly so obvious to him. ''Even when we were teenagers something about you and Hawkins occasionally bugged me, Riggs, but I never could put my finger on what it was.''

''For God's sake, there's no similarity at—'' Del began.

''Dammit, Con, we don't look anything like—'' Gabe snapped at the same time.

They both stopped speaking abruptly and stared at one another. Del's frosty gaze suddenly wavered. Gabe's hard expression turned to uncertainty.

And all at once Caro realized that the choking miasma of a smoldering smudge-fire was back, this time so thick that she could hardly breathe.

''The past has become the present. The circle has come around,'' she whispered, a nameless dread filling her. ''Dear God, if Leo wants to destroy Del, what better way could he find than to—''

She didn't finish her sentence. Instead she turned and ran from the kitchen, flying up the stairs and down the hall to the bedroom where Emily was sleeping.

Except, Emily wasn't sleeping in the crib beside the bed. Emily wasn't in the room at all. Emily was gone, the only clue to her disappearance the gently billowing curtains at the half-open window.

Terror gripping her, Caro was only dimly aware of Gabe entering the room behind her and his curse as he took in the scene.

"What better way could Leo find to destroy Del than to take his *granddaughter?*" she rasped, her knees giving way as Gabe's arms went swiftly around her.

"GABE'S GOING TO FIND HER." Standing behind the chair she was sitting in at the kitchen table, Del let his hand drop onto Caro's shoulder. "He has to," he added hoarsely.

She turned a tear-ravaged face to him. "But what if he *doesn't?* What if none of them do? I shouldn't have let him persuade me to stay here and wait in case Leo calls, Del. If I was out there with the rest of them there'd be two more of us to search, because you wouldn't be stuck here guarding me!"

Her tone climbing swiftly toward panic, she half rose from her chair, and Del gently pushed her down again. "I'd feel better if I was out there combing the Double B spread, too, but Gabe's right. Leo set this up as a kidnapping, and even if he's not interested in demanding a ransom, there's every chance he'll phone just to spin his twisted game out a little longer. We need to be here to keep him talking if he does."

He raked a hand through his close-cropped hair. "Sheriff Bannerman's got volunteers covering the back roads, he and his deputies have set up roadblocks on the main routes, and thanks to Connor, the FBI's on the way. As for the Dinetah, Matt Tahe's Tribal Police have it sewn up so tight that a shadow couldn't slip past them. The other thing that's in our favor is we know Leo doesn't have more than half an hour's head start on us, since Emily was in her crib when you checked on her before coming downstairs tonight."

He was doing his best to bolster her spirits, Caro thought leadenly, but he knew, as well as she did, that if the mysterious Leo had gotten onto the Double B property, there was a possibility he could get safely off it.

*After all, a baby wouldn't slow him down much,* she thought, her hands clasped together tightly on the table. *And if he found Emily was hampering his escape, a monster like Leo wouldn't have any qualms about—*

"Whatever you're thinking, put it out of your head." Del's voice was sharp enough to break through her fearful imaginings. He covered her hands with his. "I know it's hard not to, sweetheart," he went on gruffly. "But if you try to stay strong for me, I'll do my darnedest to stay strong for you. Deal?"

"Deal," she answered unevenly, feeling a sudden rush of affection for the tough ex-marine. She forced a shaky smile. "Tell— Tell me about Mary Morgan, Del. If you want to, that is," she added.

His smile was as much of an effort as hers, but he didn't seem offended by her request. "I don't mind. Mary's one of the few good memories I have of that time. I told Greta about her the second time we went out together."

Momentarily his gaze darkened. "Sure hope she's fit to come home from the hospital tomorrow," he muttered. "Can you believe I used to think of myself as a loner? I didn't realize that woman was my soul until I almost lost her a couple of months ago."

He took a breath. "But that's another story, and you were asking about Mary. She was Navajo, of course, and like I told you before, she wouldn't let me quit my rehab, not even when I was at my lowest. Greta once said that if Mary were alive she'd look her up and thank her for giving me back my life."

"So you knew she'd died?"

Del nodded. "I knew she'd died. I never knew she'd given birth to a child." His jaw tightened. "Mary and I only had a single night together, but it wasn't a one-night stand for either of us. We were two shattered people reaching out for something that would give meaning to the hell we were going through. She'd found out she was a widow, and I was living with the fear that I could never be a man again. Mary proved me wrong. She likely broke every rule in the book by coming to my bed, but she gave me back my faith in myself as a man. I never knew until tonight that I'd given her what she most wanted—a child."

He brought his hand up to cover his eyes for a moment. When he brought it down, his gaze was suspiciously bright. "She left the V.A. hospital soon after. Her occasional letters stopped coming after a while, and the ones I sent to her were returned 'address unknown.' A few years later I hired a private investigator to track her down, and he found out she'd died. He asked me if I wanted him to get more information, but I told him it wasn't necessary."

"You blame yourself for that, don't you," Caro said.

"Yeah, I blame myself," Del said softly. "I blame myself for not being there for my son while he was growing up." He looked at her. "You think it's too late for us to have some kind of relationship?"

Her throat tightened. "Gabe's right—you *do* need some sense knocked into you, Lieutenant. Can't you see that the two of you already have one?"

He squeezed her hand. "Maybe we do, at that. He's given me a beautiful granddaughter, that's for sure. And he's going to bring Emily back to us, sweetheart, don't you worry—"

The shrill ringing of the wall-mounted telephone beside him drowned out the rest of his sentence. Dropping her hand, Del turned swiftly and reached for the instrument.

"Double B, Hawkins speaking." His parade-ground bark was tinged with the same electric fear that Caro could feel, but almost immediately his tense posture sagged. "Tye. No, I thought you were someone else. I don't have time to explain, but Susannah can fill you in on the situation. She's with Tess and the kids at—"

Abruptly he fell silent. As long as she and Del had

been talking together, Caro thought numbly, she'd been able to keep her terror under control. Now all that was stopping her from racing from the house and frantically screaming out her daughter's name was the knowledge that giving in to hysteria wouldn't help Emily.

He'd gained a son and lost a granddaughter in the space of an hour, she thought through her pain. What enemy from his past could hate him so much as to want to inflict such a carefully orchestrated revenge on him?

Somewhere under the blanket of fear that fogged her mind, a small part of her brain was still struggling to do its job—as if, she decided later when she reflected upon it, there was a single pinpoint of rationality inside her that knew Emily's life depended on her mother's ability to make some kind of sense of a senseless situation. It was that small part of her brain that made itself heard now.

*There are only two men in the world whose love and loyalty to Del could have turned to such corroded hatred. The man who once thought of Del as a brother, and the man who believed himself to be Del's son. Both those men are supposed to be dead…but what if one of them—*

"That was Tyler." Del hung up the phone and turned to her. "He's just come back from the morgue. It's the damnedest thing—he says that although the body the *federales* discovered was dressed in the clothes Jess was wearing when you saw him killed, it's definitely not—"

"But what if one of them *isn't?*" Caro whispered

through tense lips. She got to her feet and pushed past a startled Del. ''I'm calling Joseph Tahe at the gate. We need to find Gabe right away.''

Even as her shaking hand reached for the receiver, the phone rang out. Before Del could react, she snatched it up, barely giving the metallic voice on the other end of the line a chance to speak before she interrupted.

''The deception's over, so turn off whatever device it is you're using to disguise your voice,'' she said harshly. She fought back the nausea that was threatening to overwhelm her and gripped the phone so tightly that her knuckles whitened.

*''What have you done with Emily, Jess?''*

# Chapter Fourteen

"Crawford picked the one area of the Double B spread that the searchers might miss, for his rendezvous with us," Del muttered as the Jeep he and Caro were in—a vehicle modified for his use with hand controls replacing the foot pedals—nearly bottomed out on a slab of rock. "This whole area looks deceptively flat. You can sweep a high-powered light over it and still not see that the land dips down into this wash and then up again."

He maneuvered around another rocky slab. "But that's just as well. We can't risk anyone stumbling upon us, not after Jess's threat about what he'll do to Emily if he thinks we've double-crossed him. You'll pass on my message to Gabe for me?"

Caro didn't trust herself to speak. Mutely she nodded, fresh tears slipping down her cheeks and the nightmarish telephone conversation she'd had with Jess twenty minutes ago replaying itself in her mind.

"I haven't done anything to Emily—not yet." Even though she'd already guessed Leo's identity, at the sound of the metallically distorted tones changing in midsentence to Jess's familiar voice, she'd felt as if she'd just received a blow. "And I don't want to, Caro. You know how I feel about her."

"I know how you *said* you felt about her. When you asked me to marry you, you said you would love her as much as I did," she'd replied. Her control had broken. "Please, Jess, just let her go! If it's a hostage you want, I'll take her place!"

"I'll trade Emily's life in return for her grandfather's." Suddenly his voice was no longer familiar, but coldly distant. "You were smart enough to know that it was me making this call, but maybe you haven't figured out everything. Do you need me to tell you who I'm talking about?"

"You're talking about Del." As if Jess could see her, she'd shaken her head. "You don't want to do this. You're not a—" She'd paused. When she'd spoken again there'd been dull horror in her voice. "But of course you're a killer. I saw a man die on that truck, and the *federales* found a body dressed in your clothes. Who was he, Jess—some hitchhiker unlucky enough to bear a passing resemblance to you after your paid thugs hid half his face with a gag and a blindfold?"

He'd ignored her question. "The terms are that you and Del come alone to meet me, and although I meant what I said about not wanting to hurt Emily, if I think you've crossed me I'll kill her without a qualm, understand?"

"I—I understand," she'd replied. "Where do we meet you?"

Instead of giving the directions to her, he'd asked to speak with Del. The ex-marine's carved features as he'd taken the phone had told Caro he'd gotten the gist of the conversation from her end of it, including the identity of the caller, and he'd listened without interruption to Jess's instructions.

The Jeep jolted over another rock, and Caro glanced at Hawkins. He was going to his death, she thought. He'd accepted that fact like the marine he'd once been.

"It's me he wants, and it's me he'll get," he'd said quietly as they'd left the house. "Something obviously snapped in him when I told him that final time that I wasn't his father. He must have seen it as a rejection he could only deal with by destroying me, and he concocted this whole elaborate scheme toward that one, single-minded end. That's why I believe him when he says he'll let you and Emily go."

His jaw tightened. "Tell Greta her old mustang loved her more than she'll ever know. And tell Gabe—" He'd hesitated and then gone on, his tone low. "Tell my son he grew into the man I always thought he could be."

*And into the man I might have spent the rest of my life with,* Caro thought achingly as Del brought the Jeep to a stop, *if only I hadn't destroyed any chance of that by trying to keep his daughter from him.*

He had said she'd done the right thing. That didn't cancel out the fact that she'd broken trust with him. Something had happened to Gabe on the Dinetah tonight—something that had nothing to do with his meeting with Alice Tahe, something that she'd seen in his eyes as soon as she'd walked into the kitchen of the Double B and met his gaze. Whatever it had been, it had changed him from a strong man who'd always fought his battles alone, to an unbeatable warrior, ready to take his place as a leader of other warriors.

*He found his roots.* Even as the startled thought crossed her mind, Caro knew it was true. Gabe had come home to his roots—not only those he'd discovered on the Dinetah, but the ones nurtured so long ago on the Double B by an ex-marine who'd seen himself in the rebellious teen. And she had no one to blame but herself for the fact that the life he would grow from those roots wouldn't include her.

But it would include Emily. Gabe's father was prepared to make the ultimate sacrifice to ensure that it would.

"This is where he told us he'd be." As they exited the Jeep, Del frowned. "Like I said, this wash is hidden. But even if Crawford only uses his running lights to illuminate the scene, they'll be instantly visible to anyone on the—"

Without warning, the barren landscape of the wash was suddenly bathed in an eerie red glow. Del looked toward the now-visible shape of a parked truck and the figure advancing toward them.

"I should have guessed he'd take that into account. He's fitted his headlights with red gels to cut the glare."

Caro didn't reply. She was too busy straining her gaze for any indication of her daughter, but as Jess drew nearer she didn't see Emily in his arms.

"I was watching to make sure you weren't being followed," Jess began, but she didn't let him finish.

"Where's my child?" Only Del's restraining hand on her arm prevented her from covering the twenty or so feet separating her from the man she'd once considered marrying. "Where's *Emily,* Jess? Why isn't she with you?"

"Because I learned a thing or two about handovers from those ruffians I hired in Mexico;" he retorted. "She's in the truck, and when I'm finished here, I'll let you go to her, Caro. If I'd been carrying her, I couldn't be sure that while I was handing her over to you, Del wouldn't try something."

"And put a child and a woman in jeopardy to save my own skin?" Del's smile was wintry. "Let's get on with this, Crawford. I'm here and unarmed like you stipulated. You told me on the phone this was to be an execution, so where do you want me to stand?"

"Crawford? You only used to use our last names when you hauled us up on the carpet over something, Del."

Jess flashed the little-boy grin that Caro had seen him give so often in the past when he'd realized he'd overstepped a line. Under these circumstances, she thought sickly, it was grotesque. His grin faltered as Del remained silent.

"It didn't have to end like this. You knew how much I looked up to you when I was a kid—how much I still looked up to you. Why was it so damn important to set me straight on my belief you were my father? Why did you have to take that away from me?"

"Because what you believed wasn't the truth," Del said tersely. "And although I made my share of mistakes with the teens in my charge, lying to them was never one of them."

Caro couldn't stay quiet any longer. "For God's sake, Jess—if this is all about how much you admired and loved Del, how does killing him fit in?" she burst out. "How did you let this get so out of control?"

She shook her head in confusion, still finding it hard to reconcile the reason they were here with her memories of the man she had thought she'd known.

"I know when you take up something you sometimes let it become an obsession," she said helplessly. "Maybe that's what happened here. But at some point you must have woken up to reality and been horrified at what you were planning, even if Steve Dixon was okay with being a party to it for a price."

"Steve?" Slowly the grin spread over Jess's features again. "Man, that's sweet! I wasn't sure you'd suspect him enough to look at the books, but just on the off chance, I overrode the security systems and linked him to the Dos Abejas payouts. Hell, I created that software. The security kept out every other hacker in the world, but not me. And the bastard *was* stealing from me, you know. Crawford Solutions made Stevie a rich man, and he still couldn't resist putting his hand in the cookie jar."

"Hold on a second." For the first time since they'd arrived, Del's composure cracked slightly. "Dammit, Crawford, he admitted to everything. He used my wife as a hostage to get away. Are you trying to tell me he was innocent?"

"Like I say, the Milagro thefts were his, so no, not totally innocent." Jess shook his head. "Beats me why he would admit to the Dos Abejas ones, though. The Swiss account they went into was mine, not his. Money never was that important to me, but I'm a little too old to want to start from nothing all over again. Of course—'' he gave Caro a small smile ''—by the time the authorities get the necessary permissions from the Swiss banking authorities, that particular account will have been closed out.''

She didn't smile back at him. ''As soon as we showed Dixon those payouts—payouts he knew he hadn't made—he must have realized that the only person who could have framed him like that was you, and that somehow you'd faked your own death,'' she said slowly. ''He didn't run because he was guilty, he ran because he was scared of the noose he could see tightening around his neck.''

In the red glow dimly illuminating the scene it was hard to see Jess's expression. ''Steve brought it on himself,'' he retorted, ''just like Andrew Scott did. Dixon's lucky he didn't end up an unidentified body in a Mexican morgue, too.''

He shrugged. ''Scott came to me after he'd gone to the feds, and told me he'd figured out that I'd reacted the way I had when he brought the Dos Abejas payouts to my attention because I'd made them myself. He was almost as good a hacker as I am,'' Jess added with a frown. ''He said if I gave him a piece of the action, he'd disappear and the feds would never hear from their whistle-blower again. I agreed, and told him I'd give him the money at the villa in Mexico.''

Caro closed her eyes, seeing again the bound figure

in the back of the truck, seeing again the shot that she'd believed had ended Jess's life, but that had really killed the man who'd tried to blackmail him.

Beside her, Del drew in a harsh breath. "Scott deserved what he got. Dixon deserved what he got. How far does your twisted logic go, Crawford? Did Caro deserve to be run off the road by you and left for dead on the Dinetah? What did she ever do to you?"

"She gave you a granddaughter," Jess said with a crooked smile. "With the snoop software I've recently developed for certain unnamed buyers, there isn't a secret in the world I can't unearth. I knew about Mary Morgan months ago. I realized she'd borne your son, Del, and I knew that son was Gabe. I'd already pried the truth of Emily's paternity from Larry Kanin. The man's no genius, but when his ex-fiancée gave birth nine months after leaving his chalet with Gabe Riggs, even he could guess at what had happened between them. Anyway, whether you knew it or not, Caro had given you a granddaughter and that put her in your camp as far as I was concerned. You still don't understand just how much I hate you now, do you, Hawkins."

"I'm beginning to," Del said slowly. "But I don't believe it's because you finally learned I wasn't your father."

"Bravo, Lieutenant Hawkins, bravo," Jess said, an odd note in his voice. "You're right, it wasn't because I learned you weren't my father. It was—"

"*...all of us Double B's were given leave together. That shy little girl from your hometown came all the* *way out to the coast to see you, and you took her and us out to dinner one night…''*

An icy hand seemed to wrap itself around Caro's heart as Daniel Bird's words came back to her, and she completed Jess's sentence for him before he could finish.

"It was because you knew Del had *killed* your father," she said. "You're Zeke Harmon's son, aren't you, Jess. And although he was a murderer and a rapist, he was still your father and you intend to avenge his death."

"His death and his betrayal at the hands of a man he thought of as a brother," Jess replied hoarsely, the gun in his hand wavering. "He was just as much a part of Beta Beta Force as MacLeish and Daniel and yourself, Hawkins, but they turned their backs on him and you hunted him down like an animal—hunted him down and murdered him."

His voice shook. "I think I always knew you really weren't my father, but I looked up to you so much that I allowed myself to hang on to the illusion as long as possible. When you finally forced me to let go of the lie I'd been telling myself all my life, I knew it was time to find out the truth. You'll never know how I felt when I realized that the man I'd idolized for so long had been responsible for my real father's death."

"Harmon was a killer," Del said incredulously. "For God's sake, Jess, he raped your mother! If I hunted him down like an animal, it was because he'd turned into one."

"He was a Double B!" Jess said thickly. "I'm the

son of a Double B, dammit, just as much as Gabe is!
But you took that away from me, Hawkins, and now
you're going to have to answer to *me* for what you
did in the jungle all those years ago!''

The gun in his hand came swiftly up. Caro caught
a glimpse of his face, contorted with pain and mad-
ness, and saw the gleam of tears in his eyes as he
began to pull the trigger.

''This one's for my father—''

Jess fell bonelessly to the ground, the huge hunting
knife in his back still quivering from its flight. From
the shadows behind him stepped a figure.

''I'll take it from here, son,'' said the figure, bending swiftly and dislodging the knife from Jess's back.
He straightened up and turned a nightmarish visage
toward Del.

''Hello, Lieutenant Hawkins,'' he said in a voice
that to a frozen Caro sounded familiar, clogged as if
there were stones grating together in his throat. ''It's
taken me over thirty years...but finally I've reunited
with my old Beta Beta Force brother-in-arms again.''

Caro stared in horror at the man she knew as her
sinister rescuer from the fire on the Dinetah, the man
Alice Tahe knew as Skinwalker...and the man, she
realized in dawning terror, that Del had known as
Zeke Harmon.

*''UNTIL A MAN KNOWS where to find his soul, how can
he keep it safe?''*

Gabe Riggs finally had the answer to the question
Alice Tahe had asked him earlier that evening. ''You
can't, Grandmother,'' he said under his breath. ''You

can't, so you have to learn the hard way just how big a fool you've been. You have to find out that the woman who's the very soul of you is somewhere out there in the night with a killer on the loose. And by then, there's a chance you've found out too late.''

Gabe paused, the darkness pressing in all around him. He bent down and brushed his fingertips lightly along the scrubby grass that grew here on this isolated portion of the Double B property. Rubbing his fingers together, he felt the residue of leaked oil from Del's ancient Jeep—the residue he'd been tracking by touch since the telltale black drips that he'd noticed in the glare of his headlights on the road leading from the house to the west pasture had abruptly veered off, and he'd continued following them on foot.

He was still on their trail, thank God. He kept going.

Half an hour ago he'd returned to the house to see if there'd been any word from Leo. He'd stood in the middle of the Double B's empty kitchen and felt cold dread slice through him at the realization that Caro and Del were gone. In that moment, the words he'd spoken to her this morning had echoed mockingly in his mind.

He had told her he'd decided to go back to the job. He'd assured her that he would see her and Emily several times a year. He'd presented his plan to her as if he was offering a future between them, but really he'd been offering her no kind of future at all.

*Because you were too damn scared to, weren't you,* he told himself savagely. *Face it, Riggs—since the moment you saw her at Larry Kanin's chalet, you've*

*known in your heart that if you had a future with any
woman, that woman was Caro. But having a future
with Caro meant commitment, and commitment meant
you couldn't remain a loner. And remaining a loner
was the best excuse you could give yourself for not
coming back to the Double B and making peace with
who you are.*

So, yeah, he'd been scared, he admitted as he bent
again and brushed his fingertips along the grass. The
first time he'd been so damn scared he'd ended up in
the desert, with the memory of her haunting his
dreams. The second time had been even worse, because by then he'd realized how much he wanted to
take that final step with her. He had said the words.
He had seen the pain in her eyes. And he had known
he'd just lost her.

Telling himself she had been the one who'd destroyed any hope of a future between them by with-
holding the truth about Emily had worked for a while.
But he'd returned from the Dinetah a changed man,
even if he wasn't sure how that change had come
about, and he hadn't been able to lie to himself any
longer.

He hadn't been able to lie…but he still hadn't let
himself acknowledge the whole truth. That had only
come to him as he'd stood in the empty Double B
kitchen and known that if anything happened to Caro,
his soul would be lost.

Gabe reached down again, but instead of touching
grass, this time he barked his knuckles against a slab
of rock. The rock was covered in oil. Slowly he
straightened, every nerve in his body on sudden alert,

and as he did he thought he could see a faint reddish glow coming from just ahead of him, where the terrain dipped down into a dry wash.

A moment later he was on his belly, inching forward toward the rim of the incline. He raised his head to look over it…and heard the voice of a dead man.

''This one's for my father—''

From his vantage point fifty feet up, Gabe saw Jess crash to the ground, and for one confused moment held himself responsible for the instantaneous death he'd just witnessed. The shotgun scabbard on his back was empty, the weapon itself was in his hands and he was sighting down the barrel of it, although he'd drawn it with such reflexive speed he had no firm recollection of his actions. But his finger was still on the trigger and the trigger hadn't yet been pulled. He eased off on it. Only then did he see the hilt of the knife protruding from Jess's body.

*Jess's body?* That shock was more than he dared puzzle over right now, Gabe told himself. He had to get to Caro and his daughter—from the crying he could hear coming from Jess's parked truck, it was obvious that Emily was in the vehicle. All he really needed to know at this point was that somehow Jess hadn't been killed on a lonely road in Mexico two weeks previously, but had been alive up until a few seconds ago—alive and, judging from the gun he'd been pointing at Del, acting out a murderous agenda of his own.

*Which means that whoever threw that knife just saved Del's life,* he told himself edgily. *Except, I don't think I'll run down there just yet to thank him.*

*In fact, I think I'll tighten up on this trigger finger again and—*

A man came from the shadows behind Jess, stooped swiftly and retrieved the knife, saying something in an oddly hoarse tone that Gabe couldn't catch. The man turned to Del, and this time Gabe did hear the words.

"It's taken me over thirty years, but finally I've reunited with my old Beta Beta Force brother-in-arms again."

Maybe if he hadn't just seen another man who was supposed to be dead, his mind might have fought against accepting that the tall figure with the horrifically scarred face confronting Del and Caro had to be Zeke Harmon, Gabe thought, a cold calm settling over him. But if one ghost had threatened the Double B tonight, why the hell not two?

He steadied the shotgun.

*"No!"*

Icy sweat broke out on his brow and instantly he swung the barrel of his weapon to one side. In the split second that Del had shouted out his protest at Harmon and that the man grabbed Caro and laid the blade of his knife against her throat, it had been Caro's terrified face that appeared in the sights of his shotgun.

*He can't know I'm here. But he was once part of a crack covert-ops team, and he's instinctively shielding himself from the one piece of terrain that an enemy might aim from,* Gabe thought, fear gripping him at the sight of the blade gleaming against Caro's skin. *So I'm going to have to go down there to get him.*

And he didn't have much time, he realized, beginning to move in a running crouch down the side of the wash, as Harmon addressed Del.

"Thirty-odd years is a long time, Lieutenant. Long enough for a man to work out the perfect plan, especially if most of the other ways men find to fill their time are no longer available to him. The booby-trap bomb I rigged that took your legs didn't leave me with much of a face, as you see—although I admit I came off better than you, and a lot better than the nameless soldier I killed and exchanged ID tags with, to be identified as me by the authorities. But from that day forward I was forced to live my life under cover of darkness, to hide my hideousness from the world."

"Let the woman go, Zeke," Del said steadily. "She has nothing to do with this. This is Beta Beta Force business."

Halfway down the slope, Gabe felt a pebble dislodge itself under his shoe. He froze, his gaze on Harmon. The man instantly stiffened and raised his head as if testing the air for any scent of danger.

"*...an evil that walks like a man and talks like a man. But this evil is no man, it is a ghost. He means to bring death to all you hold dear...*"

"You were right, Grandmother," Gabe breathed, as Harmon turned his attention back to Del. "He calls himself Zeke Harmon, but your ancestors and mine would have recognized him for what he is—a Skinwalker. If you can hear me now, pray that this Dineh warrior's aim is true when the moment comes to slay this evil."

"No, Lieutenant, my business with you is personal. And the woman is very much a part of it…the woman and the child, both."

In the eerie reddish glow, it seemed to Gabe, as he risked a glance, that Harmon's grin looked blood-stained. Harmon continued. "That's the perfect revenge I came up with—for you to see your grand-daughter and the woman who might have been your daughter-in-law die before you do. Why else would I have saved your life a few minutes ago, and the woman's when my son tried to kill her on the Dine-tah?"

"You've made a terrible mistake."

Caro's tone was shaky but clear, and at the sound of it cold fear sluiced through Gabe. *Don't provoke him, princess,* he begged her silently, raising the shot-gun and then lowering again, unable to get a clear shot.

"Emily isn't Del's granddaughter. I don't know how you would have gotten that idea, but surely now that you—"

"Oh, pretty mama, it's going to be a real shame slitting that slim throat of yours." Harmon shook his head, seemingly in regret. "But I guess I'll have to be content with the memento I took from you last time. I liked you better with long hair, you know," he added. Without warning, his voice hardened. "Do you think I don't know all there is to know about my enemy? After thirty years of living in the shadows, I have methods and contacts you couldn't even imag-ine. The child is Hawkins's granddaughter, and if there was any doubt of that, your conversation with my son confirmed it. All you have left now is a choice, Lieutenant. Who dies in front of you first—pretty mama here, or the little one?''

''That's not his choice, that's *mine*.'' Caro's words were strained. Her neck still arched backward and the knife poised by her jugular, she slanted her gaze sideways at her captor.

Harmon shifted his position slightly, and frustration edged Gabe's nerves. It was as if the man *could* sense his presence, he thought, cautiously circling closer to the truck. Every time it seemed an opportunity was about to present itself for a clear shot that wouldn't risk Caro's life, Harmon moved just enough to keep her head in front of his.

*And a head shot is what you've got to get here,* Gabe told himself sharply. *Anything less, and that bastard will kill her before he falls.*

''I'm Emily's mother, so it's my choice to make. I choose to die before my child does,'' Caro said, her gaze still on Harmon. ''Do you want to know why? It's because I'll die knowing I bought her a few more minutes of life—and that in those few minutes, help could arrive.''

Her eyes blazed blue out of her white face. ''Even if the cavalry came charging over that hill right now, I'd insist on seeing my daughter safe before anyone made a move toward me, do you understand, Harmon?'' Her lips pressed together. ''But of course, you don't. Despite your rape of Jess's mother, you were never a parent, and only a mother would know how I feel—a mother…or a *father*.''

*Harmon has the senses of a wolf, but he doesn't*

*know I'm here,* Gabe thought. *Del doesn't, either, and neither can Caro. But although she can't know, she hopes I'm somewhere I can hear her—because what she said just now was meant for me, not Harmon.*

She wanted him to go to their daughter before he did anything else. She didn't know what she was asking. Even if everything went wrong—*and it's not going to,* he told himself grimly—and his shot missed Harmon, the man wouldn't be able to make it here to the truck to snatch Emily before a second round took him down. It just wasn't humanly possible to—

But what about Zeke Harmon was even faintly human anymore? Gabe thought, fear flashing through him. If there was a chance in a million that one hair of Emily's head could be harmed by the thing that Alice Tahe called Skinwalker, could he afford to take that chance?

"Then, that's how it'll be, pretty mama. Lieutenant, we were once a band of brothers—you, me, Bird and MacLeish. We all bore the same tattoo of two bees fighting to the death and it was supposed to symbolize that any one of us would die defending another..."

"Yah-ta-hey, my daughter," Gabe said softly as he reached into the back seat of the truck and lifted Emily into his arms. "It's your daddy, come to dry your tears. But first we need to get your mom."

She'd been quietly grizzling, her tiny face wet with tears, but at his whisper she fell silent. Gabe dropped a quick kiss on the top of her dark curls and began to creep out of the shadow of the truck, alert to the least indication that Harmon's words to Del were drawing to an end.

"…Bird and MacLeish were followers. That didn't mean they didn't deserve retribution, but when the plans I made for them didn't turn out the way I'd hoped, I didn't waste time in trying again," Harmon said in his hoarse voice.

He had to be talking about the recent incidents at the Double B that had targeted Susannah and Tess, and through them Daniel Bird and John MacLeish, Gabe thought as he moved cautiously closer, Emily in the crook of one arm and his shotgun ready to be brought instantly into firing position in his other hand. He saw Del's gaze flick from Harmon to Emily and then back again, and he felt his heart skip a beat.

*Don't try it, Hawkins,* he thought fearfully. *He'll kill her before you could jump him, and you know it. Just hang tight, Dad, and let me get that one clear shot I need.*

"But you, Lieutenant—you were my commanding officer. I would have gone to hell and back for you, and I always thought you would do the same for me. Instead you handed me over to the authorities, and when I escaped you came after me to kill me."

"You had to be stopped, Harmon," Del said emotionlessly. "And as for going to hell, you sent yourself there when you stopped being a marine and became a monster."

"And now I'm sending you, Lieutenant," Harmon rasped. "But you'll go there screaming at the sight of your granddaughter's and her mother's deaths."

The scar tissue that surrounded his mouth stretched

into a smile. Still pulling Caro's head back by her hair, he put her slightly away from him. The blade of the knife at her throat gleamed red in the eerie light.

"You destroyed me once, Hawkins. Now I'm destroying you. The past has become the present—"

*"And the circle has come around, Harmon,"* Gabe said harshly, stepping out of the shadows as he brought the shotgun up and fired.

He'd needed one clear shot, he thought as, holding his startled but uncrying daughter tightly to him, he ran toward Caro. He'd gotten that one shot, and his aim had been true.

Harmon's lifeless body lay on the ground in front of Del. Even as Gabe reached Caro and drew her a few feet away, he saw his father strip off his jacket and throw it over what had been Harmon's head before turning aside with a grimace.

"Emily—is she all right?" Caro's gaze had been blank with shock. Now momentary fear replaced the blankness, and Gabe hastened to reassure her.

"She's fine, princess. Not a scratch on her, although I think she's none too happy about her daddy shaking like a leaf while he's holding her. Maybe— Maybe you'd better take her from me."

"How did you find us? How did you know where Emily was? Did you—" Caro's stream of questions abruptly halted. She stared up at Gabe, tears flooding her eyes as she held her daughter to her breast. "You *are* shaking," she whispered unsteadily. "Why?"

"Because I knew I had one chance to save my soul, sweetheart," he replied hoarsely. "And I was so afraid I might lose the woman I love before I could ask her if she'd marry me.''

"Son, if you're heading up to a proposal, I'd say you've got maybe two seconds to get it out before the whole damn Double B contingent sweeps down on us.''

Glancing upward at Del's laconic comment, Gabe saw several sets of headlights come to a stop at the top of the rise. He gave his father a wry grin.

"Sir, yes, sir,'' he drawled, before meeting Caro's gaze again. "We can get into details and explanations about what just happened here later, honey,'' he said. "Right now, I think I'll take the advice of a crusty old ex-marine and cut to the chase. I want a future with you, Caro—a future with you and my daughter and maybe a few more children. That future's going to be right here on the Double B, if you don't mind becoming a ranch wife. Marry me, princess?''

"Only as soon as I can, Riggs,'' Caro whispered raggedly, a brilliant smile lighting up the sheen of happy tears in her eyes before she closed them and rose up on her tiptoes.

"Only as soon as we can,'' Gabe agreed, his mouth coming down on hers.

# Epilogue

"Greta looks positively glowing. I don't know why none of us guessed she might be pregnant," Caro said to her brand-new husband. She glanced happily around the flower-festooned yard of the Double B where their wedding guests, including Alice Tahe, were enjoying themselves. "Thank goodness the tests she had at the hospital last month all came back fine."

"Dixon didn't get too far before the feds caught him, did he," Gabe said. He winced. "You realize I'm going to have a little brother or sister? That's not so bad, I guess, but Del's so thrilled about it, he's almost insufferable. If I hear one more veiled reference to Greta's old mustang again…"

He grinned at her, shifting a sleeping Emily in his arms. "I'm happy for my father. I'm happy for Con and Tess, too, with the little one they're expecting. Tye and Susannah say they want a few months of baby Danny sleeping right through the night before they consider an addition to the family, but I wouldn't be surprised if Daniel Bird becomes a grandfather for the second time sooner than he thinks."

Caro gave a sigh of pure contentment. "It must be

something in the water. Did you run your idea past Connor and Tyler?''

''About us taking over Recoveries International and basing it here, at the Double B?'' Gabe nodded. ''They said to count them in, princess. Neither of them wants to leave the ranch, but let's face it, with the millions Del got from the sale of Crawford Solutions, he and Daniel and MacLeish aren't only going to be able to expand the teen boot-camp operation, but they're talking of taking on more help. Con and Tye felt the time was right to strike out on their own with me.''

''It still seems unbelievable that Jess didn't change his will when he turned against Del, but I suppose he assumed that wouldn't be necessary, given his plan. Del was right when he said the best use for that money was to build futures for the teens who are sent here.'' Caro's gaze darkened. ''Harmon and his son Jess both did their best to destroy what the Double B has come to stand for. They didn't realize that when the two generations of men who cared about this place joined together, the force for good you created could never be defeated.''

She shook her head and the somberness in her gaze was replaced with mischievous happiness. Leaning closer to the man she loved, she murmured into his ear. ''But let's get back to talking about babies and pregnancies and futures. You're not the only one who's going to get a new little brother or sister in the coming year, Gabe. Emily is, too—eight and a half months from now.''

Incredulous joy spread over his face. ''You mean you're—we're—''

Gabriel Riggs had come home, Caro thought lovingly as Gabe, his voice too full of emotion to continue, gathered her tightly to his chest.

And home was a place called the Double B…

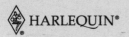

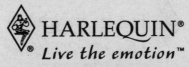

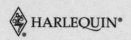

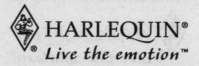

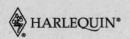

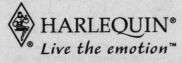

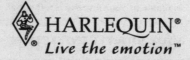

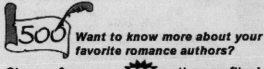

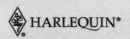
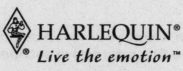